BABIES for the BILLIONAIRE

JUDY ANGELO

THE BILLIONAIRE BROTHERS KENT

Book 2

BAD BOY BILLIONAIRES
Volume 1 – Tamed by the Billionaire
Volume 2 – Maid in the USA
Volume 3 - Billionaire's Captive Bride
Volume 4 - Dangerous Deception
Volume 5 - To Tame a Tycoon
Volume 6 - Sweet Seduction
Volume 7 - Daddy by December
Volume 8 - To Catch a Man (in 30 Days or Less)
Volume 9 – Bedding Her Billionaire Boss
Volume 10 - Her Indecent Proposal
Volume 11 - So Much Trouble When She Walked In
Volume 12 – Married by Midnight
THE BILLIONAIRE BROTHERS KENT
Book 1 - The Billionaire Next Door
Book 2 - Babies for the Billionaire
Book 3 - Billionaire's Blackmail Bride
Book 4 - Bossing the Billionaire
COLLECTIONS
BAD BOY BILLIONAIRES, Coll. I - Vols. 1 - 4
BAD BOY BILLIONAIRES, Coll. II - Vols. 5 - 8
BAD BOY BILLIONAIRES, Coll. III - Vols. 9 - 12
THE BILLIONAIRE BROS. KENT - Books 1 - 4
BAD BOY BILLIONAIRES, Double Coll. - Vols. 1 - 8
BAD BOY BILLIONAIRES, Mega Coll. - Vols. 1 - 12
HOLIDAY EDITIONS
Rome for the Holidays - Novella
Rome for Always - Full-length Novel
The NAUGHTY AND NICE Series
Volume 1 - Naughty by Nature
THE CASTILLOS
Book 1 - Beauty and the Beastly Billionaire
Book 2 – Training the Tycoon

Book 3 – The Mogul's Maiden Mistress
Book 4 – Eva and the Extreme Executive
COMEDY, CONFLICT & ROMANCE Series
Book 1 – Taming the Fury
Book 2 – Outwitting the Wolf
judyangeloauthor@gmail.com

BABIES for the BILLIONAIRE

ANYA PETERSEN has always been described as gentle, understanding and quiet. The last thing she'd be called is a bully. But when a certain handsome stranger walks into her life her defense instincts go into overdrive, and she does whatever it takes to protect her heart - by keeping him far away from her. Then he turns up in the last place she would expect - and that's when she knows, where the battle for her heart is concerned, she's already lost the fight.

Rafe Kent is so entranced by the German beauty he meets while touring Europe that he will do anything it takes to be with her, even if it means moving halfway across the world. But there's no way he could have known that getting close to the woman who's stolen his heart would mean he'd need a crash course in handling tiny tots...and fast!

(Note: Gentle pacing; heavy petting scene; no consummation)

CHAPTER ONE

"RISE AND SHINE, YOU bum."

Rafe groaned at the much-too-cheerful voice of his roommate. Crap. Why did he have to be in such a good mood all the time? Trying to ignore his pain-in-the-ass friend, he reached for the extra pillow and dragged it over his head. No way was he going to be up at the crack of dawn, not for love or money.

He snuggled deeper into the bedclothes, gearing up to go his second lap on the sleep train, when the blanket was ripped off his curled-up form, the pillow yanked off his head. Before he could so much as shift, the pillow slammed into his head - not once but two times then three.

And then, all hell broke loose.

"Pillow fight!"

Rafe didn't stand a chance. Like dogs gone wild, the other occupants in the tiny hostel room jumped into the melee, and with Khalil in the lead, they beat him down until all he could do was wrap his arms around his head and hunch down low.

But Rafe wasn't going out like that. Swift as a cat, he rolled out of the low bunk bed, dropped onto the floor and grabbed the first ankle he could reach, upending its owner onto the floor with a thud.

In a flash, he was rolling across the floor, grabbing occupant number two and giving him the same treatment. He'd pushed up onto his knees and was heading for his final victim, but the kid was fast. He dashed toward the bunk bed and was soon up on top and out of Rafe's reach.

"Ugh." Khalil groaned from where he lay on his back. "You didn't have to be so violent, man." With another groan, he rolled over onto his knees then stumbled to his feet.

"Yeah, what's with you?" Lion shook his head, his long blond dreadlocks slapping his face with every move. "Can't you take a joke?" His normally pale face now red, he reached out to grab the edge of the narrow bed and pull himself up into a sitting position.

Only the kid who'd bunked in their room that night looked happy. And he had every reason to be. He'd escaped Rafe's revenge attack and now sat staring down at them, his grin stretching from ear to ear.

Rafe gave the kid a cool stare then a slow nod, letting him know he'd been lucky to get away. Then, satisfied he'd suitably punished the key culprits, he got to his feet and lifted his arms in a long stretch. When his arms fell back to his sides he was ready for the day.

Ignoring the kid, he glared at his friends. "You guys need to start acting your age. A pillow fight? Leave that to the teenagers." Then he shrugged. "Heck, even they would scoff at this kind of stuff."

Still rubbing his tailbone, Khalil staggered over to his bed on the top bunk. "You talk like we're old," he said with a snort. "It wasn't that long since we left Princeton. I don't know about you, but I don't call twenty-nine old." He shoved his hand under his pillow, pulled out his wallet and stuffed it into his back pocket.

Lion was up now, and he barked out a laugh as he jerked his chin toward Rafe. "And he's not even as old as we are. Just turned twenty-six a few months back."

"Twenty-eight," Rafe reminded him, "and that's not the point. What kind of example are we setting for this kid here?"

Lion, as if just remembering the stranger in their midst, peered up at the young man as he watched them from his perch. "What's your name, kid?"

"The name is Carlos," the boy said, his heavily accented voice a lot deeper than what anyone would expect from someone with a baby face like his. "And I'm no kid." He shifted on the bed till he was sitting up, his legs dangling over the edge and his head almost touching the ceiling. "I'm the oldest one in this room."

That got him a snort from Khalil and a chuckle from Rafe. "Yeah," Khalil said. "In your dreams."

That made Carlos give him an amused smile then he pushed himself up from the bed and dropped, limber and smooth, to the floor. "I'm thirty-three years old, gentlemen. A senior to all three of you."

Rafe's brows lifted in surprise. "You could pass for fourteen."

Carlos chuckled. "Not the first time I've heard that. It's because I'm small-boned, and no matter how I pray, my face stays as smooth as a baby's bottom."

Rafe folded his arms across his chest. "You're sure you're not fourteen?"

Carlos laughed. "You can ask my congregation back in San Jose. I'm sure they'll vouch for me."

"Congre...what?" Lion, who'd been busy digging through his duffle bag, looked up. "You're a church man?"

Another laugh from Carlos. "You could say that. I'm a minister and I'm on my way to Rothenberg to help set up our newest missionary post."

"Well, I'll be..." Lion looked incredulous. "A minister of religion bunking with us. You shoulda told us, man. If we'd known we wouldn't have been so raucous last night."

Khalil wasn't so quick to accept the story. He cocked his head to one side as he listened. "If you're a minister like you say, why didn't you fly to this Rothenberg you say you're going to? A minister trekking across Germany with nothing but a backpack? I'm not buying it."

Carlos shrugged. "Let's just say there wasn't much room in the church kitty for air travel. And besides, I wanted to do it this way so I could meet people along the way. I like to get a feel for the place, you see. And anyway," he was turning as he spoke, reaching for the knapsack he'd used as his pillow, "it doesn't matter what you believe. I know what I'm here for," he turned back to them, "and gentlemen, since I have a job to do, I'll be on my way."

Carlos set the knapsack on his back, gave them a smile and a polite nod, and headed toward the door. "God speed, gentlemen," was his farewell and then he was gone.

"Damn," Khalil said, looking like he finally believed. "A minister of religion in a pillow fight."

"Yeah," Rafe said with a sarcastic snort. "They're just like regular people. Who'd have thought it?"

"Aaw, shaddup." The frequent victim of Rafe's sarcasm, Khalil aimed a punch at his arm but missed when his target easily sidestepped the blow.

"He's a man on a mission," Lion said, looking thoughtful. "A serious fellow who knows why he's here."

"Yeah," Khalil said, with a grin. "Not like two and a half aimless fools with nothing better to do than go backpacking across Europe."

"Two and a half?" Rafe asked, curious.

"Yeah. You, Lion and only half of me. The other half's a real serious dude, just like the guy who just left here."

Rafe cocked an eyebrow. "Is that right? What's the serious half? The part that quit his job at the snap of a finger and decided to come trekking with us?"

Khalil laughed. "Yeah, that half. That was the best decision I ever made. That Wall Street job was sucking the soul out of me. Money, money, everything money. The way those cats carry on, you'd think there was nothing more to life." Then his face turned thoughtful. "Know what? Of the three of us I may be the biggest fool. After all, with my good job I had the most to lose but I still think it was the best thing for me to do. We've been talking about this since college. I'm glad I came."

"No time like the present, right?" Lion walked over and gave him a hearty slap on the shoulder.

"Yeah, before you get stuck with wife, kids and a mortgage payment." Rafe's lips twisted in a cynical smile. "Almost been there, almost done that. Lucky for me it didn't work out."

Lion looked at him askance. "What? The wife and kids? I know you're not scared off by a lil' ole mortgage. Where you're concerned, who needs one?"

"Yeah, yeah." Rafe shrugged him off then busied himself digging through his bag for his toothbrush and towel. "I'm heading for the shower. Catch you guys later."

And as he headed down the narrow corridor of the travelers' hostel, he couldn't help but wonder if his brothers were right. In fact, his whole family thought he was sort of crazy. After all, what other men with his kind of wealth would be hiking across Europe with only what he could fit into a rucksack? On top of that, as his oldest brother would always remind him, he was almost thirty, for God's sake. Ransom was always hounding him, demanding to know when he was going to settle down and take his online software company seriously.

But that wasn't Rafe. As long as there was a world to explore, there was no way he was going to tie himself down to one place, to one business or, for that matter, to one woman.

He smiled as that thought crossed his mind. They'd gone through France and Spain already and were now halfway across Germany. They'd met some of Europe's most beautiful women along the way. And the summer was still young. Who knew what beautiful *Madchen* would catch his eyes next?

He'd heard stories about the beautiful ladies in the next city they planned to touch and right then all he could think was, Düsseldorf, here we come.

. . ❧ . .

"Fraulein Petersen, Fraulein Petersen, er hat es wieder getan."

Anya turned at Becky's wail. "In English, Becky," she said with a gentle smile as she reached down to straighten the little girl's collar. "Remember, we only speak in English during school time, all right?"

Becky gave her a little pout, but then she nodded. "All right, *Fraulein* P...I mean, Miss Petersen. But he did it again. Hans keeps pulling my hair." And she folded her arms in front of her and turned to give her grinning tormentor the evilest look a five-year-old ever could.

"Hans, did you pull Becky's ponytail?" Anya gave the child the sternest look she could manage but how tough could you be with a tiny boy who obviously had taken a liking to his petulant classmate?

"Ja, fraulein," he said, admitting his sin without hesitation, "but only because it hit me in the eye."

"It did not." Becky's retort came quick and cutting. "He's just naughty, Miss Petersen. Punish him."

"All right, Becky. We'll deal with that when we get back to class. Now, fall in line, you two. We have to keep up with the rest of the class." Anya shooed them along, hurrying to catch up to the two teachers who were guiding the rest of the kindergarten class as they gazed in wonder at the Humboldt penguins waddling about on the flat rocks then diving into the shimmering pond below.

Zoo am Meer Bremerhaven was a popular venue for children of all ages and the teachers at Coleman Private English school did not hesitate to take full advantage of its proximity to the school. Today, the kindergarten class was out exploring the aquarium, gazing at the underwater creatures. They oohed and aahed when the seals and the Northern gannets dove underwater, and when the polar bear did the same, they all clapped in glee.

Although the children were having fun, the teachers knew that, at that age, a couple of hours of this adventure was as much as they could take. Soon, it was time for a bathroom break, and then they were heading back outdoors where there was ample space for the children to burn off some energy. After that, they could rest at the picnic tables scattered across the lawn.

"Lunch time," Anya called out, and everyone came running, everyone except Little Miss Petulant, who refused to sit anywhere near Hans Muller. "Over here, Becky. You may sit beside Peter."

Becky seemed to consider that for a moment, then, with a nonchalant shrug, she sauntered over to the towheaded boy waving at her.

"Want piece of my apple?" the little boy asked.

But Becky seemed in no mood to be friendly that morning. Not to boys, anyway. "I don't want no apple," she muttered, then folded her little arms and began to pout.

"I have grapes." Marisela pushed her bowl toward her classmate. "You like grapes."

Becky perked up. "Okay." And she slid closer to her friend, widening the distance between her and the closest boy. Obviously, after the episode with Hans, she was not taking any chances with boys.

Anya only smiled and shook her head, then she sent Freda over to keep Peter's company. Becky was wary of little boys right now but the tides would turn soon enough. The teenage years were not that far away. She would be happy for the attention then, but thankfully, that time was still another decade or so away.

Anya loved children, and the kindergarteners were perfect for her, old enough to display their individual personalities, but still young enough to be babied. She'd never had any interest in teaching in the high school system, so she'd pursued early childhood education, and when a position became available at the Coleman School, she'd quickly applied. It was her first job out of college, and she loved it.

She was smiling as she gathered up the stragglers and soon she had everyone seated at the table. "Fruits and vegetables first, children," she reminded them as they unpacked their lunch kits. "If you have chips or cookies you may have them only after you've had your fruits."

"Otto, did you hear what Miss Petersen said?" Magda Schmidt turned a stern eye on the little boy who was busy unwrapping a candy bar. "Please put that away. In fact, I'll hold on to it for you." She plucked it from his fingers. "Now let's take a bite from one of these nice, crunchy carrot sticks. Come on, they're good and healthy for you."

As Anya moved around the table, helping the other children unpack, she bit back a smile. Didn't Mrs. Schmidt know better? If you wanted a child to eat something, the last thing you should tell him was that it was healthy.

Once everyone was settled, she walked over to stand with Mary Connelly, the intern who'd joined them a month earlier. "They should be ready for their naps when we get back," she whispered. "After all this walking, they'll be out in no time."

"I look forward to it," Mary said, with a sigh. "I'm probably more tired than they are. Blimey, walking is hard work."

Anya chuckled. "I know, but the school bus will be here soon. We'll all be glad to get back and get some rest."

No sooner did she say the words, than they saw the bus rolling onto the grounds of the zoo. "Nice," Mary said, her face beaming as she waved to the driver. "Now we can leave early."

As soon as the children had finished their refreshments, the three teachers helped them pack up, and then the group headed toward the parking area where the bus driver was waiting.

"Stay in line, children," Anya admonished. "Hold hands with your partner. Stay in line and stay safe." It was the little rule they followed whenever they went on outings. It had worked all during the fall semester and even in winter when they'd taken the children sledding. Now that they were in the middle of May, though, something had changed. Maybe it was the bright and cheery sunshine or maybe it was the light, fragrant breeze. Today the children were as restless as puppies.

"Not that way, Vicky. You're not a mountain goat so no rock climbing. Stay on the path, please."

Mrs. Schmidt's stern voice did the trick. Vicky came scurrying to the front of the line to stand beside her assigned partner. They'd almost loaded all the children onto the bus when Hans, who brought up the rear, turned and spied a puppy who had pulled loose from his leash and was tearing across the grassy lawn, barking madly.

"*Kleiner Hund*," he yelled, and before his teachers could react, he was off, dashing after the wayward terrier, waving his arms as he ran.

"Hans." Mrs. Schmidt's voice was sharp but either he didn't hear her, or he wasn't going to stop just because a teacher called. He'd seen the promise of fun, far more fun than getting on a bus and heading back to school, and he wasn't letting anything keep him from it. That much was clear.

Mrs. Schmidt, with her short legs and extra weight, would have no hope of catching the little boy. Mary looked too stunned to move but Anya set off after him, calling his name as she ran. "Hans Muller, you stop right there."

But by then, Hans had almost reached his goal. There was no stopping him now.

And then she saw it. Coming from behind one of the buildings was a golf cart, its driver deep in conversation on his cell phone. And heading straight into the buggy's path was Hans.

"*Halte*, Hans!" Anya's scream ripped from her throat as she picked up speed but there was no way she could reach the boy in time. And he wasn't stopping. And neither was the buggy.

Then, before she could suck in her breath for another yell, a long, lean figure broke away from the milling crowd and streaked across the grass toward the boy. In a flash he was there, lifting Hans off his feet and into the air, swinging him to safety.

Suddenly realizing what was happening, the driver dropped the cell phone and slammed on his brake, shock stamped across his face. When he saw that the child was safe, he sagged in relief, then shook his head at the near miss.

By that time, Anya was skidding to a halt in front of the stranger holding a now kicking, screaming Hans.

"*Nein,*" the child yelled. "*Lassen Sie mich.*"

"I'll let you go," the man said, "as soon as you stop squirming. Stay still or you'll hurt yourself."

It must have been the sternness in his voice, or maybe it was the sharp look in his leonine eyes, but the little boy suddenly stilled, his eyes wide, and it was only then that the man lowered him to the ground.

As soon as his feet touched earth, Hans turned as if to flee, but Anya was there to clasp him by the shoulders and pull him close. "Hans, you could have been hurt. Why did you do that?" Sagging with relief, she stooped down and turned the child to face her. "Don't you ever do anything like that again. Do you hear me?"

As if finally realizing the seriousness of his sin, Hans's face crumpled and he began to sob, and there was nothing Anya could do but gather him into her arms and comfort him. He was only a little boy, after all.

As she held him close and his shaking stilled, she looked up at her charge's rescuer, and he was standing there, tall and lean, a grave look on his face as he stared down at them.

"That was a close call," he said, his golden eyes intense. "You need to keep a close watch on your kid."

Anya's eyes widened and she clutched Hans tighter. The man couldn't have said a more hurtful thing. This child in her care could have been seriously hurt and she was already consumed with guilt. But for this man, this stranger, to point it out? It was enough to fill her with shame.

Slowly, she rose to her feet, and as much as it pained her, she did not drop her gaze.

His eyes seemed darker now, and as he looked down at her from a height that dwarfed her tall-for-a-girl five feet seven inches, his brows fell in a frown. "What the heck happened?" Contrary to what she'd thought, the way he asked the question told her he wasn't angry. He actually sounded concerned. From his accent, she could tell he was American.

"I...Hans...he saw the puppy and just ran off before we could stop him." Involuntarily, her grip tightened on the little boy's shoulders as if to ensure he didn't try that trick a second time. Thankfully, the puppy was long gone, which meant Hans would stay put. She hoped. "Thank you," she said, her voice still breathless from her run. "I really appreciate what you did. I tried to catch him but..." Her voice trailed off as the fright came back full force. What if this man hadn't come to the rescue? She couldn't bear to think about it.

"It's okay," he said, and gave her a gentle smile, almost like he was trying to reassure her. "All's well that ends well." Then, he shoved his hands deep inside his trouser pockets and this time, as he stared down at her, there was a flicker of something like regret in his eyes.

But that made no sense at all...

His mouth twisted in a wry smile, and when he spoke again, his voice was soft and just a little bit wary. "Next time, you'd better let your husband hold on to the boy."

"Husband? What hus...oh, this isn't my son. Hans is my student." She was shaking her head as she spoke and she didn't know why it was so important to her to clear up his misunderstanding, but it was.

Like a ray of sunlight breaking through the clouds, at her words, his face cleared, and his posture became visibly relaxed. "Your student." As he nodded, his smile widened. "Cool."

Anya almost frowned. Cool? What kind of response was that? But there was no time to think about that now. "I'm sorry," she said, making sure to give the stranger a grateful smile, "but we have to go. Our bus is waiting." She took the child's hand. "Thank you, again. Very much."

She was turning to go when he stopped her. "Wait. What's your name?"

Caught off guard, she answered without hesitation. "Anya. Anya Petersen."

"And I'm Rafe," he said and held out his hand.

There was nothing to do but take it. She slid her hand in his, feeling the slight calluses on his palm, knowing immediately that this man was one who worked hard for his money. He had the marks to prove it.

And she liked that. More than that, she liked the way his long fingers curled around her hand, his grip strong but surprisingly gentle, making her modify her initial impression. She'd thought his were the hands of a workman but what she felt made her think they were also the hands of an artist.

But there was no time to dwell on the feel of her hand in his. It was time to go. "Pleased to meet you, Rafe," she said, pumping his hand, and then she pulled hers from his grasp and backed away. "Thanks again." She gave him a little wave, and this time, she did turn with her little charge in tow, and then they were speeding away across the grass and back to the waiting school bus.

With the other students already on the bus, as soon as they got to the waiting vehicle Anya hustled Hans inside. Following him, she rested her foot on the bottom step, ready to board, but at the last second, she had the irresistible urge to turn.

When she did, she saw Rafe still standing on the pathway at the bottom of the grassy knoll, his hands once more in his pockets, his enigmatic eyes still glued on her.

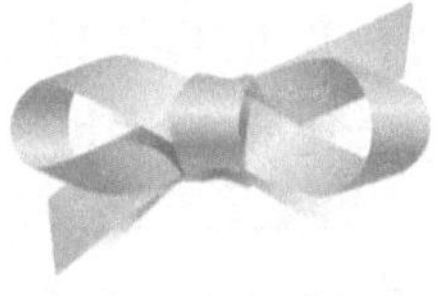

CHAPTER TWO

A GOOD TWO MINUTES later, Rafe was still standing there, staring at the school bus as it pulled out of the parking lot. "Coleman Private English School," it read. Good to know.

"Whenever you nod like that, I know you're up to something."

Rafe turned as Khalil walked up to him, a wide grin on his face.

"What crazy plan did you come up with this time?" his friend asked. "You already took us way off our route with this idea to visit towns off the beaten track. Now what new thing's on your mind?" He chuckled. "I'm almost afraid to ask."

By then, Lion had joined them. "Hey, maybe it's a good thing we didn't make it to Düsseldorf. My man Rafe got the perfect opportunity to play hero." Looking like he was impressed; he shook his head and gave Rafe a stinging slap on the shoulder.

That made him wince. "Hey, watch it, buster. Easy on the goods."

"What? I thought heroes were supposed to be tough guys. Don't tell me you even felt that." Lion's admiration quickly turned to friendly derision, just like Rafe expected.

"Yeah. It's shameful, seeing you cringe at a little slap like that." Of course, Khalil had to put in his two cents. "If she could see you now, I bet a certain little lady wouldn't be quite so impressed."

"Shut up, you two," Rafe growled, his patience with his friends running thin. Sometimes there was just so much ribbing he could take. "We were on our way to get some grub so let's do it."

"Your call, my man," Khalil said, putting his hand up. "Today, you're buying."

Rafe didn't mind that at all. In fact, if it would shut his friends up for a while, it would be more than worth it. Right then, all he wanted was some peace and quiet so he could think. And plan. And figure out how to get a certain sexy lady to go out with him.

And sexy was the perfect word to describe Miss Anya Petersen – tall and sleek and slender with sunshine-gold hair that fell in soft waves past her shoulders and hazel eyes that held you in a gaze hinting mystery and promise. He would gladly explore her depths, find the answer to that mystery and take her up on her unspoken promise. In fact, he had to. When had Rafe Kent ever passed up a challenge, especially when it involved a lovely, sensual woman with succulent lips he was dying to taste? Not to mention those long legs, perfect for wrapping round his waist.

"Snap out of it, man." It was Khalil again. "I know you're daydreaming about that *fraulein* who just caught your eye but fuggedaboutit." He started walking, heading toward the restaurant and toward food. Skinny as a rake but greedy as a mountain goat, Rafe knew Khalil had every intention of running up a huge lunch bill. At Rafe's expense, of course.

"And what's my type?" he demanded, his long legs letting him catch up to Khalil in no time. There was no way a five-foot ten shorty like Khalil could outwalk his six foot three.

His friend shrugged. "You know, the wild, adventurous type who'll match your bad behavior step for step."

Lion, who was bringing up the rear, barked out a laugh. "Bad behavior, you call it? I call it downright kinky."

That made Rafe frown. "What do you know about me and my ladies? My personal life is none of your damn business."

"Whoa. Easy now, fella. Nobody's getting all up in your business," Khalil said in Lion's defense. "But you're the one with the 'lady-killer' reputation. You've got to admit, that says a lot about you."

Rafe's response was a snort. "Maybe so, but it doesn't mean I'm kinky, so you two can just drop it." Then, he mumbled, "And stay the hell out of my business."

Sometimes, Rafe could get sensitive when they razzed him, and this was one of those times. There was a reason he went through woman after woman, discarding each along the way, but they wouldn't know that. The fact was, there'd been a special woman in his life, one he'd thought would be 'the one'. He soon found out that he'd been the world's biggest fool to think that way.

She'd used him and then she'd moved on, making her the worst kind of player there was. At least, where his women were concerned, they knew up front what they were getting into. He made no promises and they expected none. That way nobody got hurt.

And now, as luck would have it, he'd bypassed the lovely ladies of Düsseldorf and found a beautiful lily right here in Bremen. On this leg of the trip, he'd followed his nose and it had paid off. Nice.

Now, all he had to do was track her down, and with a name and a location, that was easy. His first move would be to find Coleman Private English School. His plan in place, Rafe began to feel pleased with himself. If he played his cards right, he would have pretty Miss Petersen in his bed in no time.

"Come on, slow pokes." Now, it was his turn to take a dig at his friends. "My tank is on empty. Time to fill 'er up."

It wasn't until later that evening when they'd gone back to their budget motel that Rafe got the chance to check out the Coleman School. It was on Obernstrasse. Not far at all. He made a note of the telephone number then settled back in his bed to watch the rest of the soccer game on the television. Tomorrow would come soon enough.

Next day, Rafe timed his call for twenty minutes after school dismissal time. That would give Anya enough time to get her little ones off to the school buses, or to their parents, and then make it to the teachers' staff room. It would be the end of the workday so she should be more relaxed and more inclined to take his call.

But despite his meticulous plans, when Rafe called the school office, there was no Anya to receive his call. She was probably out speaking to one of the parents, the secretary told him. Call back in about fifteen minutes. Better yet, he should just leave a message and she would pass it on. Rafe thanked her for the offer but declined. He wasn't going to risk Anya getting the message and totally ignoring it. That would be too easy for her to do. If he got to speak to her, though, there was no way she would turn him down.

Fifteen minutes later, Rafe was calling the school number again, and this time he got a much better response. "Hold on, please," the secretary said. "I will transfer you."

"Hello?" Anya's gentle voice came through the receiver, but it was hesitant, questioning.

Time to put her at ease. "Anya. It's Rafe. We met yesterday at the zoo."

"Ah, yes. Rafe. I remember." There was a pause, and he could imagine the frown on her face as she tried to figure out why the heck he was calling. As if to confirm what he was thinking, when she spoke again, it was to ask a question. "How can I help you, Rafe?" He could hear it in her voice. She was curious and she was also trying not to sound rude. Definitely a good sign. She was trying to be polite. It was these kinds of girls who were easiest to manipulate. "You can help me, Anya," he said, his voice slow, seductive and coolly confident, "by agreeing to have dinner with me." Then, he chuckled. "After all, after yesterday's experience, we're not strangers, are we?" He closed with a deliberate question designed to back her into a corner. When he worded the question like that, what else could she do but agree?

"I...no, I guess we aren't strangers," she said quickly, but still with that hint of hesitation in her voice.

He needed to dispel that doubt. "We shared a moment of danger, Anya. We're like old friends now." He spoke in his most reassuring voice. "So, how would you like to share dinner with an old friend? Tomorrow evening, seven o'clock, Medio." When there was another moment of silence on the other end of the line, he upped the ante. "I can pick you up."

"I'm sorry, I..."

Rafe knew when to jump in. Before Anya could express any doubt, he cut in, making sure to slide in that one thing the ladies could never resist. So, neither would Anya. "Say yes, and I'll throw in my personal wildcard. With that, you can demand from me anything you wish." He laughed. "Want me to do your dishes for a week? I'm your man." Then, he threw in the part that was guaranteed to make the ladies melt. "But if dishes aren't your thing, you can use me any way you want."

Rafe was still smiling as he waited for Anya's response.

It came swift and clear and surprisingly sharp. "No. Thank you. I don't think so." Anya didn't shout. She didn't need to. There was a steely coolness in her voice that told Rafe she was not the kind of woman you could trifle with.

Realizing he'd made a mess of things, he decided to try a different tactic. "Forget what I just said. That didn't come out quite the way I intended." He drew in his breath, feeling like a fish out of water. He wasn't used to this backpedalling bit. He'd used that line on so many women, and she was the first one who'd turned him down cold. He would have to approach things from another angle. Thinking fast, he said, "Anya, will you have dinner with me? After what I did yesterday it's not too much to ask, is it?"

He heard when she drew in her breath then let it out slowly. Finally, she spoke. "I'm very grateful for what you did," she said, her voice cool and quiet, "but no, I will not go out with you. Thank you again, Rafe, and have a good day."

The next thing he heard was the click that ended the call. She was gone.

Shit. He hadn't expected this. There was actually a woman who could resist his charm?

And then, even as he asked himself the question, he realized what a jerk he'd been, and what a super-jerk he was still being with that kind of thinking. Of course, Anya would turn him down. He'd approached her with the same tired line he'd used on dozens of women. But, he was beginning to realize, Anya Petersen was a different kind of woman. She'd seemed modest, easy-going, even shy, the type you could easily impress. Now he could see she was just the opposite. Anya's backbone was pure steel, the most difficult kind of woman to bend to your will.

And that, more than anything, made him want her even more.

. . ❧ . .

IT WASN'T UNTIL ANYA got home that afternoon that she got a chance to mull over her conversation with the man who called himself Rafe. He hadn't

even told her his last name, yet he'd had the audacity to think she would go out with him.

She was grateful that he'd rescued Hans and she'd told him that. Many times. Apparently, he didn't think that was enough. He'd actually asked her – no, told her – to go out with him. And then, he'd gone and made that crude remark. Such a turn-off.

Still peeved at his comment, she slammed the pot down onto the burner, making the nearby teacups rattle. Maybe she was overreacting, maybe what he'd said wasn't all that bad, or maybe...she paused and gazed out the window...maybe she'd responded so coldly because her heart had done a funny thing at the sound of his voice. For some strange reason, it had picked up pace, almost as if she were glad he'd called. But that could not be true. He was nothing to her, nothing but a kind stranger. And so, she'd remained aloof. It was the proper thing to do.

But then, as her gaze fell on the blossoming cherry tree in the garden below, her mind took her back to the previous afternoon and the image of the helpful stranger filled her mind. At first, she'd been too preoccupied with Hans to pay much attention, but once she'd reassured herself that the child was fine, she'd looked up and found herself gazing into golden eyes that glinted in the sunlight, eyes that reminded her of the flickering flames of a fire.

He was handsome, this stranger, with his wide forehead, square jaw and those intense eyes of his. She liked the way he stood tall, and she liked the way he looked, with his broad shoulders, his slender but muscular frame and the sexy curve to his legs that reminded her of the cowboys in the old movies of the wild west.

The thing that really got her attention, though, was his soot-black hair which he'd pulled back in a short ponytail tied at the back of his head with a cord made of leather. She'd seen it when he was holding the kicking boy. The way he wore his hair made him look very much the rebel. And everyone knew that the best thing to do was to stay far away from rebels.

And with that thought, Anya shook her head, a smile of regret on her lips. Her thoughts of Rafe had been nice while they'd lasted, but that was where they would have to end. She would probably never see him or hear from him again and as depressing as that thought was, that was as it should be. From here on, she would do her best never to think about that man again.

Two hours later, Anya was pulling on her sweatpants, getting ready to head out to the class she held for seniors, when there was a knock at her door. Quickly, she pulled up the pants then, still shoeless, she padded out of her room and down the hallway toward the front door. It wasn't a big house, only a tiny bungalow she'd inherited from her great aunt, so she didn't have far to walk.

She pulled the door open to find her neighbor standing on the porch, her hand on the handle of a vacuum cleaner. "*Danke schon*, Anya," she said, with a smile full of gratitude. "I'm sorry I had to impose on you, but I didn't want Karl to come home and find the house a mess."

"It's no problem, Helga. You couldn't have known your vacuum cleaner would suddenly die on you. It was my pleasure." Smiling, Anya took the handle that the woman was tilting toward her and pulled the vacuum cleaner into the hallway.

"I'll ask Karl to get mine fixed tomorrow," Helga said, her tone still apologetic. "Thank you again. I know you're rushing out, so I won't keep you."

Her neighbor seemed to be in a hurry this evening and that, Anya knew by now, was a cause for concern. "Just a second," she said, reaching out to catch Helga's hand. Slowly, she turned the woman back to face her. And that was when she saw it. As she'd suspected, Helga was sporting another bruise.

Releasing the woman's hand, she folded her arms across her chest, feeling the anger beginning to bubble inside. "What did he do this time?"

"Nothing. I swear. This was all my fault." Self consciously, she lifted her hand to the purple bruise by her left temple. She'd kept it hidden by tilting her head while she spoke to Anya, letting her hair fall over it. Now, though, she'd been forced to face front, and there was nothing she could have done to conceal her injury, nothing short of tying a scarf around her head. Clearly, she knew that would have been way too obvious. "I opened the cupboard door and then forgot." She gave a nervous giggle. "Would you believe, I turned and bumped into it?"

Anya almost gave a snort of disgust, but she held it in. Of course, she didn't believe a word of Helga's story. Karl Gruber was a known abuser and any bruise that showed up on his wife had most likely been put there by him.

And Anya was sick of it. "Helga, I'm going to say this one last time. Either you report Karl to the police, or I will."

"Now, Anya. You know I don't want you getting involved. I'll handle it." Helga was beginning to look flustered, almost angry.

"Like you've handled it every time it's happened?" Anya shook her head. "Step aside. I'm going to have a talk with that husband of yours."

Helga sucked in her breath. "Don't you dare, Anya Petersen. You just stay out of my business." With that, she whirled around and marched down the steps and down the pathway, walking fast and not looking back.

Anya could only stare after her. Finally, shaking her head, she stepped inside and closed the door, her thoughts steaming with anger and frustration.

There was nothing she would like more than to beat *Herr* Gruber into the dust. And one day, if Helga would let her, she would.

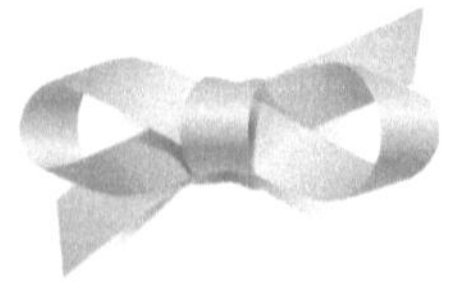

CHAPTER THREE

"WOOHOO! NOW THAT'S what I call spiffy." Lion was grinning from ear to ear.

Rafe totally ignored him, peering into the mirror as he straightened his tie. If Lion wanted to play the fool, that was his business.

"Where'd you get that suit?" Khalil asked, as he followed Lion into Rafe's motel room. "You didn't have that tucked away in your backpack, did you?"

"Nope," Rafe said, pulling back from the mirror and flexing his shoulders. "Rented it. I need to look good today. Decent."

"Dress to impress, that's what they say." Lion was looking him up and down like he was appraising a prize bull. "And today you're going to impress. Trust me."

But Khalil was frowning, looking anything but impressed. "Rented? You know you can do better than that."

Rafe shrugged. "Why should I? I'm only going to need it this once."

Lion laughed and slapped him on the shoulder. "Talk about confidence. One look and she'll be eating out of your hands, right?"

Rafe grimaced, slightly annoyed. "Right." He didn't mean that, but he didn't want to prolong the discussion. Lion was the kind of guy who would latch on to something and run with it, and Rafe had no intention of giving him any encouragement. "Listen, guys, I've got to go. I was supposed to pick up the car half an hour ago."

"You rented a car?" Khalil's sardonic look was beginning to lift. "Well, at least you're showing some class. I was beginning to wonder if you were going to hop on the bus."

"Give the guy a break," Lion said, jumping to Rafe's defense. "Just because a man has money it doesn't mean he has to flaunt it."

"Well said." Rafe gave a nod of approval. "Now, if you gentlemen will excuse me, I have a car to pick up."

"And a lady to see," Khalil said, with a knowing grin.

Lion shook his head. "Khal, for some reason, I think we're going to be in this town a lot longer than planned."

Khalil gave him a disdainful look. "Ya think?"

Rafe didn't wait to hear more. He just walked out, leaving his friends in his room. They would either chill there or head back to their own rooms. He didn't care. He had other, more interesting business to think about.

He picked up the car and got to the Coleman School a good twenty minutes before the bell was scheduled to ring. He knew, because he'd made sure to check it out online. Now, all he had to do was sit tight until dismissal time and then make his way to the main office. It had been easy for Anya to turn him down on the phone, but face to face? That would be another matter...because Rafe Kent wasn't used to being turned down.

He was flipping channels on the radio and had just landed on Radio Bremen, when the ringing of his cell phone made him groan. What did Lion and Khalil want now? If they were calling to ask him to pick up chips and soda on the way back, he would kill them.

But when he glanced at the screen, the name he saw was one that hadn't popped up in weeks. And he knew this wasn't going to be a fun call. With Ransom, it never was. His older brother could always find a reason to chew him out. Suppressing a sigh, he swiped his finger across the bottom of the screen. " 'Sup, Ran."

" 'Sup, Ran? After three weeks of silence, that's all you have to say to me?" As usual, Ransom was not in a chirpy mood. Maybe it had something to do with being in your thirties. Or maybe it was because he was a married man now. Whatever it was, Rafe wished he would lighten up.

"I was busy," Rafe said, then waited for his brother's reprimand. Ransom was thirty-five and boring as hell. This stuffy big brother of his would never understand the need to get away from the humdrum of business and just air your head out for a while.

"Busy traipsing all over Europe while your business in the United States is floundering?" Ransom's words were heavy with disgust.

"What are you talking about? I monitor my business every day and I have a competent team of managers I communicate with. What do you think a laptop and cell phone are for?"

"It's not the same, Rafe. You need to be more involved."

"I've got this, okay? I've got a CEO and a COO, for heaven's sake. What the heck do you think I pay them for?" And then, just as his annoyance with his brother began to rise, Rafe paused. "What's this all about, Ransom? Why the concern, all of a sudden?"

"All of a sudden?" Ransom gave a snort. "You've always been cause for concern. Ever since you came into my life when I was eight, you've been-"

"Yeah, yeah I know. Driving you up the wall." Rafe heaved a sigh. "So, what have I done this time?"

"It's more like what you haven't done. You haven't been staying on top of your business, and one day you're going to learn. This is not the way to run a billion-dollar enterprise. You're almost thirty, godammit. When are you going to settle down?"

"Oh, so that's what's pissing you off. I'm too old to be having fun." Rafe laughed. "Don't hate me because my business doesn't keep me tied to the ground like yours does. I wasn't built for the construction business, Ransom. That's why social media's my thing. So, I got lucky and I'm making big bucks every time people use my service to chat online. Does that mean I'm going to let it tie me to an office chair? Hell, no."

"Now, you listen to me-"

The bell rang, loud and clanging, drowning out the rest of Ransom's words. It was just as well. Rafe was tired of the conversation, anyway – the same old story about him being a renegade, the black sheep of the family, the one who refused to take his business seriously.

But no matter what Ransom or the rest of the family said, none of them could deny that he was damn successful by anybody's standards.

When the clanging stopped, he was the first to speak. It was time to end the conversation. "Listen," he said, before Ransom could get a word in, "I've got to go. Important meeting, and all that. You know how it goes." And before his brother could say anything more, he tapped on the screen and ended the call. Ransom was probably mad he hadn't had the last word. Oh, well.

But now, Rafe had other, more important things to think about, like how to get a very beautiful but reticent lady to agree to go out with him.

Feeling optimistic, he hopped out of the car and walked up the driveway leading to the school's main office, confident that he was looking decent enough to enquire after one of the teachers. At least he wasn't wearing his usual scruffy jeans, loafers and army surplus jacket. His hair was still longer than was conventional, but he'd pulled it back and tied it with an inconspicuous cord. He was neat, and that was good enough. It had better be.

When he presented himself at the office, a woman with graying hair and a friendly smile came forward to greet him. "*Wie kann ich Ihnen helfen?*"

Rafe smiled back. "You can help me by letting Miss Petersen know that she has a visitor. Please tell her that Rafe is here to see her."

The woman's smile widened. "Oh, you're American. Is Miss Petersen expecting you?"

"No, she's not. This visit is sort of...a surprise."

The woman raised her eyebrows, but her smile did not falter. "I see. Please have a seat while I call her."

Rafe didn't feel like sitting. He'd felt confident just a minute earlier but now he was wound tight as a spring. Still, knowing how intimidating his six-foot three height could be, he went over to the bench and sat. No sense in towering over the little lady who was trying to help him.

Making sure he looked cool and comfortable, he leaned back against the padded back and stretched his arms along the top. From the corner of his eye, he could see that he was the object of much attention. The ladies in the office were throwing glances his way and there were two who were whispering their heads off. None of that mattered. There was only one woman he wanted to see right then, and it was a demure damsel with wavy blonde hair.

He didn't have to wait long. Within just a few minutes, a tall, willowy woman approached, crossing the main office, heading for the reception area. It was the woman who had caught his eye, the one he was counting on to say yes.

Immediately, Rafe hopped to his feet. Anya was here. Time to show what stuff he was made of.

• • ❧ • •

"MR....RAFE. I...WHAT a pleasant surprise." Anya almost groaned. That hadn't come out quite the way she'd intended. But this visit really was a surprise, and she hadn't lied when she said it was a pleasant one. After all, this was the man who'd been on her mind all this time. And now, he was here in the flesh, and looking as tall, tanned and handsome as ever.

Even more surprising, today Rafe was looking nothing like the bohemian she'd met two days earlier. Now, he looked nothing-short of debonair in his coal-gray business suit and wine-colored silk tie. His hair was the same, though – black and shiny and slicked back. And his eyes – those eyes that had grabbed her the first time they met – now gleamed like liquid gold as he let his gaze slide up her body and to her face which she knew was probably flushed and pink. And it was all his fault. Why was he looking at her like that?

It was enough to make a girl grow moist and...she blinked. What in heavens was she doing? The man was standing right in front of her, and she was busy daydreaming about what he could do to her. Thank goodness he couldn't read minds.

"Uhm, how may I help you, Rafe?" She'd asked him that question once before, and instead of giving her a proper answer, he'd asked her out on a date. What was he up to now?

"Miss Petersen," he said, giving her a very slow, very charming smile as he approached the reception counter. "I'd like to start over, if you don't mind. I want to introduce myself properly. My name is Rafe Kent, businessman, entrepreneur, and lover of international culture." He held out his hand as if they were meeting for the very first time.

Anya bit her lip. She'd thought he was going to say, lover of women. He certainly looked the type. But then, she did a mental shrug. That wasn't fair, judging him like that. Just because he was one of the most attractive men she'd ever met, it didn't mean he was a sower of wild oats. The least she could do was give him the benefit of the doubt. So, granting him a small smile, she reached out and took his hand.

This time, instead of waiting for her to pull her hand away, he was the one who let go first.

And, despite herself, Anya could not stop the feeling of disappointment that rose inside. She was being stupid; she knew that well enough, but although she'd been the one who'd rejected him, she could not stop herself from hoping he would try again.

And then, she saw him stick his hand inside his breast pocket and pull out a business card. So, that was why he'd pulled his hand away so fast. He'd wanted to give her something. She almost smiled in relief.

"Here you go, Miss Anya," he said, as he handed her the card. "Rest assured, I'm not the beatnik I seem to be."

She took it from his fingers, a shiny ivory and gold card with the words, Kent Software Communications. She'd never heard of it, but his business was legitimate, she guessed. In any case, she could always go online and check him out. She slid the card into her pocket. Later, she would do just that.

And then he shoved his hands deep inside his pockets, and for a moment, he looked uncertain. "I was wondering," he said, "if you would join me for a late lunch. I know you're a busy woman, but even busy women have to take a break to eat." Then, he gave her a crooked smile. "Unless you're a cyborg."

His attempt at a joke made her relax. "I can assure you, I'm not. I doubt a cyborg's tummy would growl when she's hungry."

"Great. So, you'll have lunch with me?"

"I didn't say that" was her quick response. "All I said was-"

"Oh, go ahead. We can survive without you in the staff room this one afternoon."

Anya turned to see the smiling face of the woman who served as both receptionist and secretary at the small school. "Why, *Frau* Schuler," she said, surprised, "are you encouraging me to go out with someone I hardly know?"

The lady nodded, seeming totally oblivious to the fact that she'd just interrupted a private conversation. "Just take separate cars, Anya. And eat in a public place. You will be all right."

That made Anya lift an eyebrow.

"If you want to get ahead in life," Mrs. Schuler persisted, "you have to take chances. Go for it." Then, the woman patted her on the shoulder and ambled away, leaving both Rafe and Anya staring after her.

When she turned back to face Rafe, Anya was laughing. "I guess I have no choice. The 'boss' has spoken."

That made Rafe laugh, too, and then he was waving at the woman who had helped him out. "*Danke, Frau* Schuler. I owe you one."

The mood lightened, Anya didn't have it in her to say no to Rafe this time. After Mrs. Schuler had intervened, how could she? In fact, she didn't want to say no. There was nothing she wanted more than to get to know the handsome man who had gone out of his way to track her down.

After they'd agreed to meet at *Das Kleine Lokal* in thirty minutes, Rafe left, giving Anya the opportunity to tackle the resident matchmaker. "*Frau* Schuler, I know you've been telling me I need to get out more, but really."

"Yes, my dear. Really." The woman gave Anya more of a smirk than a smile. "You do nothing but spend all your free time with senior citizens. Go out with someone your own age, for a change." Then, she moved closer and whispered, "You never know; he may be the one."

"Oh, please," Anya said, with a laugh. "I don't think so. I hardly even know the man."

"And that's why you should go out with him," Mrs. Schuler insisted. "Get to know him. I can see the two of you ending up together. He's American, you're American. See? You already have one thing in common."

"I'm half German," Anya reminded her, but Mrs. Rosner was shaking her head as if that didn't matter at all. "I'll probably have nothing in common with the man. I won't know what to say." Anya was airing all the doubts tumbling around in her head. She was thinking of the fact that she'd never been great at conversation. Too reserved, she'd been told. What if today was more of the same? What if she came off as too quiet or too stilted? And what was she going to talk about, anyway? The more she thought about it, the more nervous she became.

"Want me to come with you?"

Startled, Anya looked up to see her co-worker standing beside her, a teasing grin on her lips.

"I can come along to give you moral support," Karen said. "Hey, if you don't want him, I'll take him."

"No," Anya said quickly. "That's quite okay." She knew Karen hadn't been joking when she said that last part. She had a reputation for going for what she wanted, and when it came to men, Karen did not play around. "I'm going," Anya said, and before Karen could invite herself along, and before any further doubts could creep into her mind, she went straight to her desk, grabbed her handbag, and headed for her Opel Astra.

Although Anya drove straight to the restaurant, not making any stops along the way, Rafe was already there. He'd ditched his tie, and with his shirt open at the collar, he was looking very relaxed. If only she could say the same for herself.

As soon as he saw her, he came forward, smiling. "Thank you for coming," he said. and there was a hint of relief in his voice that made her laugh.

"Did you think I wouldn't show up?" she asked, and her light attempt at teasing him was actually doing her some good. The tight coil inside her was beginning to unwind.

He cocked an eyebrow. "Well, there was always that possibility."

She only shook her head and smiled. When it came to men, especially those she didn't know well, she'd always been hesitant. But she'd never stood one up and she wasn't about to start now; definitely not with a man as charming and intriguing as Rafe Kent.

That afternoon, out there on the terrace of the restaurant, Anya shared a meal with a handsome gentleman, and she enjoyed every minute of it. Rafe was one of the most entertaining men she'd ever met, cracking her up with stories of his adventurous hikes in the Grand Canyon, his job working on an Alaskan oil rig, and his gig breaking in horses in a Texas rodeo. He'd even spent months in the forest of Central Africa, working as an assistant to a team of zoologists.

"You are one adventurous man," Anya told him. "When do you ever sit still?" And then a thought came to her. "I thought you said you were an entrepreneur. With all these exploits, when do you ever find the time to do that?"

"That, my dear, is where technology comes in. There are so many things you can do remotely these days, who needs to be in an office?"

She shook her head at that one. "Not with my job, though. Looking after my little ones is a hands-on job."

"A job that you're very good at," Rafe said, "one that you absolutely love. I can see it in the way your eyes sparkle when you talk about your work."

Surprised by his comment, Anya dropped her gaze, hoping he didn't notice her blush. She wasn't usually shy, but she wasn't -*

used to this attention, and it was making her just a little bit uncomfortable. She preferred things a whole lot more when he was telling her about his many unusual ventures.

"Hey, no need to be shy," he said, and then out of the blue, he reached out to capture the fingers she'd been tapping against her glass. "I meant what I said, Anya. You're a beautiful woman, inside and out. I could see that from the first day we met." He gave her fingers a gentle squeeze. "And that's why I'd like to get to know you better...if you'll let me."

And Anya didn't know what to say. The truth was, she wouldn't mind getting to know him, too, but was she being stupid to even think that? Even after having lunch with him, he was still a virtual stranger. But he was still holding her hand, and he was gazing at her, waiting for her answer. Finally, she spoke, but when she said the words, they sounded hesitant and uncertain. "I'll think about it," she said softly, as she tried to pull her hand back, wanting to break his grasp, wanting to regain some distance between them so she could think.

It was the strangest thing. On the phone, she'd been so sure of herself, putting him in his place without so much as a stumble. But now? Now that she was within touching distance of him, now that he was holding her hand, the firm and resolute Anya Petersen had fled, and in her place was a woman whose heart was pumping at the feel of his fingers on hers, whose mouth had gone dry at the glimpse of the dark hairs on his chest. Now, she was a woman who was totally aware, physically and otherwise, of the gorgeous man gazing at her with amber eyes.

Never breaking his gaze, Rafe nodded. "That's all I ask," he said, his voice silky and seductive. "Just think about it. But don't take too long." Only then, did he release her fingers and sit back in his chair, giving her that distance she needed to regain control.

By the time Rafe called for the check, Anya was breathing easier, and when he walked her to her car, she was almost back to normal. When they parted, it was with her promise to call him next day.

That evening when Anya got to the seniors' center to teach her class, she was still distracted. It wasn't easy to forget a man like Rafe. As much as she tried to push him to the back of her mind, she could not.

"So, who is he?" a strident voice asked, pulling her out of her reverie. "Who's this man you've been thinking about all evening?"

As Anya turned to face the elderly woman who stood there, hands on her hips, she raised her eyebrows. Was she that obvious? "What do you mean, Edith?" she asked, with a shake of her head. "Does a girl have to have a man on her mind all the time?"

Edith laughed. "No, but this girl does. You've been in a daze all evening. Hasn't she, ladies?"

"That is true," Ursula chimed in. "I was showing her my choke hold on Magda and she didn't even look."

That made Anya feel awful. For the hour and a half they were together these ladies were her responsibility and should be her sole focus. Instead, she'd been daydreaming about a man.

"But that's okay, dear," Edith said, giving her a reassuring smile. "You're such a wonderful girl, spending your time with a bunch of old ladies, teaching us how to be strong."

"And fierce," Janet piped up, grinning as she flexed her arms.

"Yes, yes, Janet." Edith waved her off. "Let me finish." Then, she turned her attention back to Anya. "I want you to find a nice man to settle down with, one who can give you lots of beautiful babies."

That made Anya laugh. "I've already got lots of babies, Edith. Sometimes more than I can handle. A whole classroom full of them."

"That's different, so don't bring it up," Ursula scolded. "Those are your students, and they don't count. We want real babies."

Anya knew exactly what she meant. Like so many other women, it was her dream to one day find that special man to love and cherish. And yes, she did want babies of her very own.

But Rafe Kent? She'd only just met him, but there was no denying that spark between them. If she ever dared feed that fire, she knew it would erupt into a blaze.

But Rafe was not the 'settling down' kind. She could tell. She had the distinct feeling he would be a dangerous one to like.

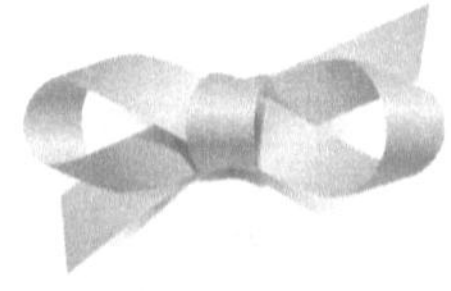

CHAPTER FOUR

RAFE COULD HAVE KICKED himself. The minute Ransom called him, he should have known something was up. His older brother had a nose for this sort of thing. From miles away, he could smell something fishy.

Now that he was back in his motel room with no hazel-eyed honey to distract him, he'd pulled out his laptop and gone online to do his daily check on the business. Everything looked good until he read the e-mail from Bert Cameron, his chief financial officer. What surprised him wasn't that he was getting an email from Bert, but that he hadn't copied his superior, the chief executive officer and, for Bert, that was way out of character. The man was a stickler for following office protocol to the letter. so what was different all of a sudden?

Rafe clicked on the link to open up the e-mail. "Mr. Kent, it is important that I bring a matter to your attention; it is one of great sensitivity. I do not wish to relay this information by e-mail. I would appreciate your calling me at your earliest conenience."

Immediately, Rafe reached for his phone. Right then, it was late morning in the United States, a good time to call Bert.

His employee picked up on the third ring. "Cameron here. How may I help you?"

"Bert, it's Rafe. I got your message. What's up?"

"Rafe." Bert sounded surprised. "Your call came in as an unknown number. I'm in office right now but could you call me back in ten minutes?"

"Ten minutes," Rafe said, and none too pleased, he hung up the phone. After sending him a cryptic e-mail like that, Bert was keeping him in suspense?

When he called back minutes later, the CFO sounded more relaxed. "I'm downstairs, just outside the lobby," he said. "I didn't want to talk while I was in my office. Walls have ears, you know."

"Yeah," Rafe said, his tone abrupt. "What's going on?"

"You're not going to like this, but I've been getting some strange requests from Michael lately."

Rafe frowned. "Requests like what?"

"Like the other day," Bert said, "he asked me to write a check to a company I'd never heard of."

"I assume an invoice was presented," Rafe countered. "You could have used that information to check if the company was legit."

"That's the thing," Bert said, his voice tinged with concern. "I found all the usual stuff – location, type of business, directors. What I didn't expect to find was Michael's name tucked away in an inconspicuous list of advisors."

Rafe's frown deepened. "You're sure it was Michael Allen, our CEO?"

"The same. I thought I'd made a mistake but when I dug deeper, I found out it was our guy." He made a clucking sound into the phone. "Talk about a conflict of interest."

"Are you sure about this?" The last thing Rafe wanted to do was to accuse a man wrongly. On the other hand, if Michael Allen was taking advantage of his position, using it to fill the coffers of his own company, he would have to put a stop to it immediately. He wasn't running his business to fill another man's pockets.

"I'm sure about this one instance," Bert told him. "Now, as far as checks I've been writing over the past year or two, I don't know, but this situation makes me wonder if he sneaked anything else in." He sighed. "Now, I'm not sure what to do about this payment."

When Rafe spoke, his voice was brittle and firm. "Stall him," he said. "Tell him the check should be in next week's batch. Let's give ourselves time to look into this further."

"I'm on it. I'll gather all the relevant data from the past two years and present them to you within a week."

"Good. And good looking out for the business, Bert. I owe you one."

When Rafe hung up the phone, he shook his head, still stunned at what he'd just learned. So, his team wasn't as trustworthy as he'd thought. This was definitely not something he would be sharing with Ransom any time soon. He was in no mood for lectures and 'I told you so's.'"

He was just closing his laptop when there was a rap at the door. He got up off the bed and walked across the room then opened up to find Lion lounging against the doorjamb and Khalil looking retro in a colorful nineteen-seventies dashiki shirt.

Rafe couldn't help but chuckle. "Where'd you find that getup?"

"Don't you worry about that," Khalil said, pushing past him and walking into the room. "How come you didn't report to us when you got back from your lunch date?"

Rafe could have been offended at Khalil's nosy enquiry, but he let it slide. Even if Rafe slammed him, it would roll off the guy like water off a duck's back.

Lion, on the other hand, was concerned with something totally different. "Did you bring back anything? Dessert? A doggy bag? I'm starving."

Rafe folded his arms and shook his head but there was a grin on his lips. "So, if I don't show up you don't eat?"

Lion shrugged. "I can't help it if I'm always broke."

"Yes, you can help it," Rafe responded, not swerved by his declaration. "If you wouldn't waste all your cash on cigarettes, you'd be good."

"Yeah, I know." Lion looked unapologetic. "So, what are you saying about the food? Got any?"

"Of course, I don't. Does it look like I have anything?" He waited, letting Lion scan the room. It was only when the man's face fell that he relented. "I've still got the car. Come on. We'll go to Kiefert and I'll get you guys some chow."

It was while they were eating that Khalil used the opportunity to ply Rafe with questions. "So, what's your new lady love like? She's nice, right? She doesn't look like the stuck-up type."

"Was she all over you," Lion asked, his mouth full of fries, "when she found out you're not some poor beggar?"

Khalil laughed. "Yeah, not a vagrant like us two."

"Speak for yourself, buster," Lion grumbled. "I'm a responsible member of society."

Khalil gave him a sardonic grin. "Says the man who just bummed lunch off his travel partner."

"Like you're not guilty of the same," Lion said smugly, then finished off the fries on his plate and turned his attention back to Rafe. "So when are we going to meet her? Like, officially. With formal introduction and everything."

Rafe cocked an eyebrow at him. "Me? Introduce Anya to you guys? I don't think so."

"Why the hell not?" Khalil looked peeved. "You introduced us to those girls you met in all the other cities. So, what's so special about this one?"

"Anya is...different. You wouldn't understand." Rafe shook his head. He'd almost said he didn't understand it, either. Khalil was right when he'd mentioned those other girls. Rafe had gone through a few of them along the way, but none had held his interest long enough to make him stay in town longer than a couple of days. But Anya? Well, all he could say was that if it took all summer to get her to like him, then he was more than prepared to stay put. When it came to heading back to Washington, he was in no hurry.

"Okay," Khalil said. "Make us understand. I want to get to know this little lady who's bewitched you."

"Me, too." Lion patted the breast pocket of his army-green vest, but when he saw Rafe's pointed glare, he dropped his hand with a guilty look. "Leave me alone, will you? I can't help it if I have a craving." Then, he leaned back in his chair and clasped his hands behind his head. "Why don't you see if she'll do lunch with you again? Then you can invite me and Khalil along."

"Sounds good to me." Khalil jumped in before Rafe could even respond. "What time should we be ready?"

"Hey, hold up, you two. Didn't I just say I don't want to introduce her to you?"

"Why not?" Khalil demanded. "Ashamed of us or something? So, we're good enough to trek all over Europe with, but not good enough to meet your princess, Miss Anya?"

Rafe gave him a cool stare, even as his friend's dark eyes flashed with each word he spoke. Khalil was a good buddy but, in Rafe's opinion, he was also way too sensitive. Too quick to take everything as a slight, that was Khalil. Lion, on the other hand, wouldn't know an insult if it hauled off and slapped him in the face. These two were as different as night and day.

"Shut up, will you?" Rafe stared Khalil down until he dropped his gaze and looked away. "I'm proud to call you guys my friends, and you know it."

"So, why don't you want us to meet Anya?" Lion asked, prolonging a discussion that would have been better abandoned.

Rafe sighed. "Because..." he glared at Lion and then at Khalil, "...I know you two. Before you know it, one of you will be trying to convince her to go out with you."

Khalil gave a dramatic gasp. "I'm appalled that you would have such a low opinion of your friends."

Rafe's gaze narrowed as he looked back at him. "It's not like you haven't done it before. Before we left Spain, Paulina came and told me all about your little charade." At the time, Rafe had laughed it off. He hadn't even let on to Khalil that he knew his friend had approached Paulina. He'd just shrugged it off and moved on, but now that Khalil was acting all holy and righteous, he decided to drop it in there.

Now, instead of his usual smirk, Khalil squirmed and dropped his eyes. "She told you about that?" he mumbled. "It was no big deal, man. I didn't think you liked her that much."

"No, I didn't like her that much, as you put it. She and I, we were just cool. But that's not the point." Rafe's brows fell. "I don't want you making moves on any woman I've shown interest in, and most definitely not this one." He folded his arms and glared. "I forgave that slip-up. Don't think I'm going to be that generous again."

Khalil looked like if the earth could swallow him up, he would gladly jump in. Saying not another word, he looked away, then nodded.

"Yeah, so about lunch…" Lion looked at Rafe, expectant. It was like he was oblivious to the tension that sizzled at the table. "How does tomorrow look? If we're doing anything, we'd better get cracking. It's not like we're going to be in this city too much longer."

"You're a trip; you know that?" Rafe shook his head, tired of Lion's insistence. "All right, I'll ask her, okay? But there's no guarantee she'll say yes."

"Cool." Lion nodded. "But I'm not dolling up in suit and tie for anybody. What say we do a picnic in the park? She might like that."

"I doubt it," Rafe said drily, "but I'll ask. With you guys not having much in the way of decent clothes, that might just be the way to go."

Lion laughed. "Like your clothes are any better. Don't get all high and mighty just because you rented a suit."

Khalil, the tightness in his face easing just a little, gave them a wan smile. "Clothes? Never your strong point, Rafe."

"True word," Lion said, and slapped his palm down onto the table. "Now, let's go for a walk. I've got to work off some of this food. I'm so full, I can only waddle."

Next day, Anya called Rafe as promised, and to his surprise, she readily accepted his invitation to picnic with his friends.

"Sure you can handle it?" he asked, teasing her. "They're not an easy bunch." It was like he was hoping she'd say no, let's just do this by ourselves. But no, she was not turned off. Just the opposite. She seemed to enjoy his attempted scare tactic and took it as a challenge.

"I'll be there," Anya said, with a laugh. "I'm yet to meet a bunch of tourists I can't handle."

And so it was that Rafe got his next date with pretty Anya Petersen. The only problem was, he would have his travel buddies tagging along. But, if that was what it would take to see her again, then he would gladly suffer their presence.

The more Rafe thought about the idea of the picnic, the more he liked it. Maybe it was a good thing Lion had suggested this no-frills outdoor luncheon. Now, there would be no need to dress up – and that was a relief, because he wasn't exactly the suit and tie sort.

Now, Anya would get to know the real Rafe Kent.

. . ❧ . .

ANYA WAS SMILING – no, grinning was a more accurate description – as she hopped into her car and entered the Autobahn on the way to Bremen Burgerpark. It was going to be a great Saturday because she was going to see Rafe again. She was in such a good mood, she felt like singing. It was corny, of course, but what could she say? She couldn't help it if she was feeling like a lovesick schoolgirl.

She pulled into the parking lot, tucked her cell phone into her pocket, and ran around to the trunk to grab the cooler. She'd offered to bring sandwiches, but Rafe had told her everything was under control. She should just bring herself. When she'd insisted, he'd finally relented and told her she could bring some drinks, and that was exactly what she'd done. She only hoped he wasn't expecting any alcoholic beverages. She wasn't a beer drinker herself and all she'd brought were bottles of water and a variety of fruit juices. For good measure, she'd thrown in a bottle of sparkling grape juice. So, she was boring. If Rafe and his friends didn't like it, they could just sue her.

Grinning as the rebel in her threatened to spill over, she hauled the cooler out of the car and headed toward the grassy knoll where they'd agreed to meet. She was halfway there when a tall, lean figure – by now quite familiar – came toward her. On his face was a wide smile.

"You're early," Rafe said, as he came close then took the container from her hands. "I wanted to meet you by your car. You shouldn't be lugging this load all the way up here."

"Oh, please," she said, flexing her arms. "What do you think I have all these muscles for?"

Rafe looked at her arms and then he whistled. "Looking good. Toned, firm. I can see that you work out."

She chuckled, a bit embarrassed at his admiration. "I try."

Then, he eased the pressure when he jerked his head toward a shady tree where a colorful quilt was spread out. "Come on. That's our spot. Take a load off."

And so, with Rafe leading the way, Anya set off toward the venue of her very second date with him. Was this only the second one? She was beginning to feel so comfortable with him, it was like she'd known him months, and not just a few days.

As they got to the tree and Rafe deposited the cooler on top of the cloth, Anya looked around. "So, where are your friends?" she asked. "Scared of little ol' me?"

Rafe laughed. "I wish. They're getting the food from the car. They'll be over in a little while. Too soon, if you ask me."

Anya shook her head. "Meanie. What kind of thing is that to say about your friends?"

Rafe was good enough to give her a contrite smile. "Put it down to jealousy," he said quietly, almost seriously. "I don't want to share you with anyone."

That made Anya drop her gaze and pretend to pick a leaf off the leg of her jeans. Rafe sounded like he'd meant what he'd said, and it made her just a little bit nervous. But he liked her. That much was obvious, and she couldn't have been happier.

"Make yourself comfortable," he said, and when she plopped down on one end of the quilt, he set the cooler in the middle, then came over and sat right beside her.

Anya's lips curled in a smile. Talk about marking your territory. His friends wouldn't be able to get close to her, even if they tried.

She jumped when Rafe leaned in close and fixed his gold-flecked eyes on her. "So, tell me all about Anya Petersen," he said. "Tell me everything, before those nosy parkers get back."

Not knowing where to start, Anya gave a nervous laugh. "I thought I told you everything when we went to lunch."

"No," he said, with a shake of his head. "You only scratched the surface." Then, as if to reassure her, he gave her a crooked smile. "What I know about you could fit in a nutshell. You're a schoolteacher, you've been at your job two years, and you love what you do. Your English is perfect because your mother is American and still lives in New York, and your father, who is German, lives in Bonn. Your parents are divorced, you're an only child, and you grew up shuttling between the east coast and Europe, taking turns with each parent." He paused to draw breath. "Did I miss anything?"

She chuckled. "No, you pretty much covered everything. There's not much more to tell outside of that."

He gave her a smile that told her he didn't believe it, but then he tilted his head even closer and looked at her with hooded eyes. "Is there a secret Anya Petersen I should know about?"

That made her laugh out loud. "You make me sound so mysterious. It's like I could have a secret life full of intrigue." She shook her head. "Trust me, I'm as boring as they come."

He didn't answer, but she could see that he wanted to say more. In fact, he looked like he wanted to do more. A whole lot more. Rafe was looking at her like he wanted to kiss her.

And, as out of character as that would be for her, she would not mind at all if he did.

Maybe she had the power of telepathy or maybe he could read minds, she didn't know which. All she knew was, at the same time her body tilted involuntarily toward Rafe, he was leaning toward her, too.

Feeling like she was moving in slow motion, almost like she was in a dream, Anya didn't stop tilting until her face was mere inches away from Rafe's. Then, of their own accord, her eyelids closed. She held her breath, waiting for his next move.

As her body yearned for his touch, Anya sensed Rafe moving closer, closing the gap between them. And then, so softly, so gently, his lips touched hers. Like the caress of a butterfly's wing, his lips brushed against her lips, sending a tantalizing thrill racing through her. She sighed.

As if taking the soft sound as invitation, Rafe's tentative touch became bolder, and he leaned in even closer, taking full possession of her lips, kissing her as if, for the longest time, he'd been dying to do just that.

Melting against him, Anya moaned, and lifted her hands to clasp his shoulders, steadying herself, clinging to him as he swept her away with his expert kiss. When, moments later, he drew back, it was too soon. Unable to hide her disappointment, she sighed and lowered her face. Her hands sliding off his strong shoulders, she clasped her fingers in her lap and finally opened her eyes.

When she did, it was to find him gazing down at her, his lips curled in a mischievous smile. "That kind of kiss," he said softly, "was not a kiss from a woman I'd call boring." His smile deepened. "It left me wanting so much more."

It wasn't what he said, but the way he said it, that made Anya drop her gaze again. She could feel the telltale pink of a blush creep up her neck to color her cheeks. The way he'd said the words in that husky, sexy voice of his made her tingle inside. There was no doubt about it. This man knew exactly how to turn a girl on. And that, as she'd suspected, made him a dangerous man indeed.

Wanting to break the spell Rafe had cast over her, the one that made her lower her defenses, Anya cleared her throat then looked around, desperate to find something else to talk about, something that would break the tension that made her so aware of him. She was glancing around when her gaze fell on two men heading in their direction. One, a tall, pale figure with long twists of blond hair falling almost to his waist, was carrying a huge picnic basket, while the other, almost his polar opposite, with dark skin and a huge afro, carried a couple of big, brown grocery bags.

"Are those your friends?" she asked, tilting her head toward the men.

Rafe turned to follow the direction of her gaze. "Yup. Here comes the food."

Rafe was saying the right words, but he didn't sound eager, like she'd expected. The whole point of a picnic was the food, right? When it came to Rafe, though, it didn't seem like that was the case. And she knew exactly how he felt...because she was feeling the same way, too. |Just then, food was not exactly at the forefront of her mind.

But now, Rafe's friends were standing right in front of them. Time to push her attraction for Rafe to the back of her mind. Time to paste a smile on her lips and get ready for introductions.

Rafe got to his feet then gave her his hand and helped her up. As she stood beside him, he casually threw his arm across her shoulder and pulled her against him in a move she could only describe as possessive. "Anya," he said, "meet Lion and Khalil, my travel mates."

"And long-time friends," the pale one said, as he dropped the big basket onto the quilt, then wiped his palm on the seat of his khaki trousers and stuck his hand out to her. "I'm Lion," he said. "Good to meet you, Anya."

"And I'm Khalil," the other friend said, with a cautious smile which made her wonder if he was scared of her. Although, why he would be, she had no idea.

"Pleased to meet you, Lion," she said, taking his hand. "And you, too, Khalil." She gave him a reassuring smile. "I'm happy to meet both of you."

The introductions over, Rafe took her hand again and helped her back to the quilt-covered ground. Then, he turned his attention to the booty his friends had just brought. "Did you get everything?" he asked. "I could eat a horse and I'm sure Anya's starving, too."

Anya only smiled. Rafe was exaggerating, of course. It wasn't like they'd been sitting there, anxiously awaiting the arrival of the food. They'd been occupied with other, more stimulating things.

Lion flopped down beside the basket and lifted the lid. "We've got fried chicken, bread rolls, coleslaw, salad and salad dressing. And, I would have you know, we have potato salad. Everything present and accounted for, captain."

"Don't forget the dessert," Khalil said, finding a spot next to Lion. "We got a pound cake and some fruit salad. All bases covered."

Rafe nodded, looking satisfied. "Sounds good. Especially the potato salad part." Then, he bent his tall, lean frame and relaxed by Anya's side.

Khalil shook his head. "What it is with you and potato salad, I'll never figure out." He turned his dark-eyed gaze on Anya. "Can you believe the man made us go all the way back to town to hunt down potato salad? We ended up going to three stores before we found any."

The man looked so disgruntled that Anya had to laugh. "I'm sorry he put you through all that," she said. "I'll make sure he behaves from now on." And even as the words left her mouth, she couldn't believe she'd said them. She'd made it sound like she was going to be around him that long. As it was, she didn't even know how long he would be in Bremen. And although she had absolutely no right to feel that way, the thought made her feel just a little bit depressed.

"Okay, Mommy, I'll be good." From where he lay, propped up on his elbow, Rafe turned his face up to her and gave her such a chastened look that she laughed. It was exactly what she needed to put her back in a cheerful mood.

Rafe sat up then dug into one of the grocery bags and pulled out a pack of paper plates. "Now that it's settled that I'm going to be a good boy, let's eat."

"Hear, hear," Lion said, rubbing his hands together in a comical display of eagerness.

Khalil, who seemed to be the most serious of the lot, took the plates from Rafe and proceeded to use huge plastic spoons to ladle out potato salad, coleslaw and vegetable salad onto each one. As he handed the first plate to Anya, he tilted his chin toward a huge metal fork in the basket. "Grab that and stab whichever piece of chicken suits your fancy," he said. "People can be particular when it comes to chicken. Take Rafe now. He's strictly a breast man. Me, I eat anything."

It was stupid of her, but when he said that, Anya had to bite her lip to keep from giggling. So, Rafe was a 'breast man'. Well, she hoped that only applied to his taste in chicken because if that was what he looked for in a woman, with her, he was out of luck.

"So, what do you like, Anya?" Rafe asked, as she held the fork over the basket.

She gave him an impish smile. "I'm a dark meat kind of girl," she said, then stabbed the fork into a particularly juicy-looking chicken leg, lifted it and dropped it in the middle of her plate.

"Me, too, girl," Lion crowed and grabbed himself a chicken leg. He didn't even wait for her to pass him the fork. He just grabbed the drumstick, put it to his mouth, and chomped down. "Mmm," he moaned, eyes closed. "This place makes some good chicken." He stretched out the word 'good' so long that Anya could only smile. He was obviously enjoying his food.

But when she turned to glance at Rafe, her smile faltered. Instead of laughing at Lion's antics, like she was, his face had turned dark; so serious that she almost asked him if something was wrong.

But then, as quickly as his look had turned sour, his face cleared, and he was grinning back at her. She must have been imagining things.

"Here you go, Rafe." Khalil held the basket out to him and then he helped himself to a chicken breast.

Soon, they were all busy with their meals, enjoying the food and the balmy breeze under the Kentucky Yellowwood tree. The conversation was light and funny, and Anya found herself laughing so hard she began to worry they'd think she was tipsy. Although tipsy from what, she couldn't say. It wasn't like she'd been drinking anything stronger than grape juice. The only thing that could come close to making her tipsy was a certain handsome fellow who was lounging beside her, lying so close that his leg was touching hers. He probably didn't even notice, but as innocent as it was, it held a hint of intimacy that had her thinking thoughts that were admittedly inappropriate. Oh, if only she could keep her mind on the casual banter. *Come on, Anya. Focus.*

"So, what's the hardest part about traveling with Rafe?" she asked, trying to start a conversation thread that would distract her from the leisurely sensuality of the man who lay beside her.

"I can answer that," Lion piped up, just before he stuffed the last piece of pound cake into his mouth.

"Hey, no more talk about me," Rafe said, looking like he was glad Lion's mouth was too full for him to speak. "You've already embarrassed the heck out of me. Enough already."

"Never enough," Anya said, egging Lion on. "Rafe's told me so much about his adventures, but only the good parts. I want to know about the real Rafe Kent, good and bad. Tell me more."

"Don't encourage him," Rafe growled, but it was too late. By then Lion had swallowed the last of the cake and was looking like he was ready to roll. Talking was definitely his thing.

"Rafe," he said, his gray eyes sparkling with mischief, "is the pickiest person when it comes to..." A cell phone rang, cutting him off midstream.

"Sorry, guys," Rafe said, digging into his pocket. "It's mine." When he glanced at the screen, he frowned. "I've got to take this. Excuse me a minute." He tapped the screen to answer the phone, then got up and put the device to his ear. "Speak."

As Rafe walked across the grass and away from them, Khalil shook his head. "Don't expect him back any time soon. From the look of things, it's going to be a while."

"Yeah, so where was I?" Lion asked with a shrug. "Oh, yeah. We were talking about Rafe's bad habits."

Anya gave him a tiny frown. "I don't know if we should talk about that when he's not here."

"Why not? It's not like I'm saying anything I wouldn't say to his face." Lion rolled over onto his stomach like he was getting super comfortable. "Yeah, he's picky," he continued, "when it comes to food. It makes life on the road really tough when we can't find the right kind of food for Rafe. I remember this one time in Brittany, we went to four restaurants before he found one that did his baked salmon just right." He shook his head. "Picky, picky, picky. I wish he'd be as picky with his women, as he is with his food."

Anya's head jerked up. She was just in time to see Khalil give Lion a warning glare. "What did you just say?" Her voice was deceptively cool.

"I...nothing. I just..." Lion's voice trailed off, and he glanced at Khalil as if for support.

But Anya was having none of it. He'd made a comment that demanded an explanation. So, Rafe wasn't picky with his women? What did that mean? He'd found a love interest at every stop, and she was just one among many? "Why would you say something like that?" she asked, her voice soft and amiable, reflecting none of the fire that was beginning to burn inside. She even managed a small smile. "What did you mean?"

Now Lion was beginning to look really uncomfortable. "It was nothing," he said with a shrug, but the color that was slowly creeping up his neck belied his casual tone. "I just meant, he shouldn't be quite so popular, that's all."

"Popular with the ladies, right?" She gave him a pointed look.

"Yeah," he said slowly, practically groaning the word. "But it's not what you might think. It's just that he had this girlfriend, right? And she hurt him, so ever since then, he's got this policy where he just-"

"I got this, Lion." Khalil broke in just when his friend's babbling would have given Anya the information she needed, the information that would have told her who Rafe Kent really was. "Don't pay any attention to what Lion said, Anya." Khalil gave her a grave look. "Rafe's a really cool guy. There's nothing about him you need to be concerned about."

Anya looked at him askance. "You're his friend. I don't expect you to say otherwise."

"I'm telling you the truth," he said, looking annoyed that she'd had the audacity to question what he'd said. "Don't judge him by what Lion said. Lion just talks too much sometimes."

"You're right." To Anya's surprise Lion was actually agreeing with Khalil. Instead of looking upset that his friend had called him a virtual blabbermouth, he looked contrite. "I always talk too much and sometimes it ends up getting me in some deep doo-doo." He sighed. "Like now."

Anya didn't say a thing, and neither did Khalil. In fact, he looked like he didn't intend to say a word to Lion for the rest of that afternoon.

But, in the end, Anya was glad Lion had been loose with his lips. It taught her a valuable lesson, and right in the nick of time. Just when she was beginning to really like Rafe, even harboring fantasies that he might like her enough to want to stick around in Bremen for a while, this thing happened; it dragged her back to reality. The man was a womanizer, so bad that his friend couldn't even keep from commenting on it. Rafe was the last sort of man she should ever get involved with.

So, to Rafe she was just another conquest, was she? Well, he would soon find out she was not that kind of girl.

She wouldn't even ask him to explain himself. When he came back from his call, she would just be good and gone.

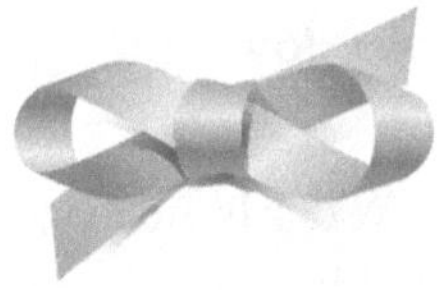

CHAPTER FIVE

RAFE WAS SHAKING HIS head as he walked across the grass, back to the picnic party. It never rained but it poured. Bert was calling much earlier than planned. He'd found even more evidence of Michael's transgressions. On top of that, it was now looking like there was an insider, someone within Rafe's company who was helping Michael embezzle funds. What he'd found out, Bert surmised, was probably just the tip of the iceberg. But he needed more time, he told Rafe. Within a week, he should have enough information for Rafe to get involved. But not yet.

Rafe was mumbling to himself, lost in his thoughts, as he got back to his friends. He was about to sink down onto the quilt when he realized that Anya was not there. He looked around. "Where's Anya?" he asked, as he turned to look in the direction of the parking lot. "Did she go back to her car to get something?"

Not hearing an answer, he glanced back at his friends. "Either one of you can jump in any time. Where'd Anya go?"

Khalil glanced at Lion, and Lion looked back at Khalil. And for some strange reason, the two of them looked guilty as hell.

And Rafe couldn't explain it, but the look that his friends exchanged suddenly made him uneasy. "I'm going to ask one last time," he said, his voice cold and hard as steel. "Where the hell is Anya?"

That finally got a reaction out of them. Khalil shook his head, but Lion got up from the ground and stood with his hands stuffed deep inside his pockets. He wasn't looking at Rafe, though. His eyes were glued to the ground. He cleared his throat and then he began to speak.

"I'm sorry," he said, his voice low, "but Anya's gone. And it's all my fault."

Rafe frowned then cocked his head to one side, waiting for the explanation, but Lion had fallen silent, looking like he didn't know what else to say. "What do you mean, she's gone? Gone home?" He folded his arms across his chest. "Why did she leave? What the hell did you do this time?"

Lion lifted his shoulders, almost in a helpless gesture. "I didn't do anything," he said, sounding uncertain. "At least, not on purpose."

Rafe didn't bother with him. Instead, he turned his attention on Khalil. "What did he do?" he asked, knowing that, from Khalil, he would get nothing but the truth. "What did he tell her?"

Looking like he'd rather not say, Khalil drew in a breath, then he let it out slowly. He shook his head. "He told her you were pickier in your choice of food than in your choice of women." He threw an apologetic glance at Lion before continuing. "He didn't mean anything by it, Rafe. You know that."

"You told her what?" Rafe wasn't even listening to Khalil anymore. All he could do was stare at Lion, astounded. Could a grown man be so dim-witted? "Lion, why the devil would you do something like that? That was none of her business, dammit." He looked away, shaking his head, flummoxed by his friend's stupidity. When he looked back at Lion, he was so bewildered he couldn't even hold on to his anger. "Guys look out for one another," he said. "They don't go behind their friends' backs, giving reports to all and sundry." Then he growled, "Especially not to a girl you know your friend really likes."

Lion looked crestfallen, like Rafe had just told him their friendship was at an end. He dropped his gaze and kicked at a tuft of grass. "I didn't mean to mess things up for you," he mumbled. "All I can say is, I'm sorry." Then, he turned and walked away, down the hill and toward the distant pond.

"Don't be too hard on him. He was just talking, and it slipped out."

At Khalil's words, Rafe turned and glanced at him. "Isn't that the way it always happens? I'm sick of Lion and his blunders. Jeez, when will he ever grow up?" Then, with a hiss of annoyance, he stalked off across the grass, deliberately heading in the direction opposite to where Lion had gone. He was in no mood to forgive him or to pretend that he wasn't royally pissed.

It took almost a half hour before Rafe calmed down enough to help his buddies pack up the car and head back to town. Not surprisingly, the journey was quiet and strained. When he got to his room Rafe slammed the door shut behind him and flopped down onto the sofa facing the bed. He'd thought his phone call would have been the worst of his troubles that day. If only.

That night, he didn't see or hear from Lion or Khalil, which suited Rafe just fine. It wasn't like he was in the mood for small talk, not after he'd missed out on the chance to get to know a truly beautiful woman. And he wasn't just thinking about her physical beauty, either. Anya was the kind of woman you'd change travel plans for. She was the kind who made you want to stay put.

Trying to distract himself, even as he pondered his next move with Anya, Rafe watched wrestling into the wee hours of the morning. Next morning, he woke to a pounding on his door. Groggy and bleary-eyed, he stumbled over to pull it open to find Khalil and Lion in his doorway, both of them looking fresh-faced and obscenely wide awake.

"What's the matter with you two?" Rafe grumbled. "Why are you bugging me at this hour?" He looked from one to the other but instead of looking suitably chastened they were both grinning.

"Do you know what time it is?" Lion asked, his subdued demeanor of the previous day totally non-existent.

"Who the hell gives a damn? It's Sunday, you jerk. You don't come pounding on a man's door this early on a Sunday." Rafe drew back from the door, turned his back on the men and stumbled back into his room.

"Temper, temper," Lion chided, following Rafe into the room.

"And such language," Khalil added.

As if Rafe cared. The two of them might be in a good mood, but his mood was just as sour as it had been the day before. He threw himself back onto the bed and dragged the sheet over his head. Khalil and Lion had better entertain their own damn selves.

"Rafe, do you know what time it is?" It was Lion again, this time in an annoying singsong voice. "You may think it's still morning," he said, "but lunchtime is long gone."

His head still under the covers, Rafe frowned. Lunchtime? Had he slept that long?

"And we have good news," Lion continued. "Tell him, Khalil."

That caught Rafe's interest. He pulled down the covers and peered at his grinning friends. "Tell me what?"

Khalil cleared his throat, then sat forward in the sofa he'd been lounging on. "We have the perfect solution to your Anya Petersen dilemma," he said, his tone smug. "We did some investigation and found out that she does volunteer work with a seniors' group, and she'll be meeting at a center not far from here." He paused, as if for effect. "This very evening."

Rafe's eyes narrowed. "So? How does that help me?"

"Don't you see?" Lion piped up. "You don't have to wait till she's back at school. You can go meet her at the center."

Rafe sat up in the bed, the possibility of seeing Anya that evening making his heart pick up pace. But then, as he thought about it, his eyes narrowed. "So, you want me to come off like some kind of stalker?"

"No, man. We would never set you up like that." Khalil looked at Rafe like he should have known better. "We already talked to the little lady. She's expecting you."

"You talked...huh?" Now, Rafe was really confused. "First of all, how the heck did you find her to talk to her, and second, what in God's name did you say that would convince her to see me?"

"We have our ways," Khalil said. "Never underestimate the power of the internet."

Rafe's brows fell. "You did an internet search?"

"Yep. I did a search on Miss Anya Petersen and found her on Linked In. I found a couple of articles about her, too. Apparently, she's big on volunteer work in Bremen."

"Okay," Rafe said slowly, "but how did you find her? You said you talked to her, right?"

"He called the seniors' center featured in the article," Lion said, "and they were so nice, they gave him her number. Can you believe it?"

"No, I can't." Rafe shook his head. "That's a breach of personal privacy by anybody's standards. Why the heck would they do that?"

Lion shrugged. "Maybe because Khalil put on a fake accent and pretended to be Anya's brother from America."

"She doesn't have a brother," Rafe said, exasperated.

Khalil lifted an eyebrow and gave him a crooked grin. "I guess the sweet old lady I spoke to didn't know that. She was so nice. And she spoke pretty good English, too."

Rafe bit down on his lip. He wasn't liking the sound of this. According to his friends, they'd gotten him a second chance with Anya, but they'd done it through deceit. How would she react when she found out? Or maybe she'd figured it out already? And what would that mean? That, although she stormed off, she really wanted to see him, so it didn't matter? Rafe didn't know what to think.

"Anyway, it doesn't matter how we found her," Khalil continued. "The important thing is that she's expecting you at the center this evening, right after her session with the seniors." With that, he got up, rubbing his hands together, looking satisfied. "Well, my work here is done. You're leaving at six o'clock, Rafe. I'll come get you. Don't be late."

He sauntered out of the room with Lion in tow, leaving Rafe wondering if they'd just done him a huge favor or if they'd screwed up his chances with Anya for good. The problem was, the only way he could find out was to go to this little 'meeting' they'd arranged. If Anya turned around and slammed him for showing up, he would kill them.

That plan resolved in his mind, Rafe got out of bed and headed for the bathroom. Half the day was already gone. Now, it was time to get cracking and get productive. There were tons of things sitting on his laptop, waiting to get done, and he was never one to shirk his responsibilities, no matter what his big brother thought.

Hours later, after a late lunch he'd gobbled down in his room, Rafe was still busy on the laptop when there was a knock on his door. It was Khalil again but this time, there was no Lion playing shadow.

"It's almost time to go," he said. "Just reminding you to get yourself ready."

"I'm ready," Rafe said. "I'm just finishing up some work then I'll be good to go."

"Cool. I wrote down the address for you." Khalil walked over and deposited a small piece of paper on the night table. "S,o do you want me to tag along, or you're good?"

"I'm good. Why would I need you to come with me?"

"I don't know. Moral support, or something like that." Khalil shrugged. "I just want to make sure things work out all right this time. Of all the girls you've met on this trip, I can see you really like this one."

"Yeah, I do," Rafe said, "so no more talk about all the girls I've met. That kind of talk already got me in enough trouble."

"Right. I'll keep that under wraps." And with that, Khalil gave him a quick nod and exited the room, leaving Rafe to his preparations.

Immediately, he got up from the table where he'd been working, picked up the paper Khalil left, and stuffed it into his pocket. Then, he got the keys to the rented car.

As he walked out the door, he could only hope that things would take a turn for the better.

. . ❧ . .

"A LITTLE LOWER, EDITH. Like this." Anya made a pointy elbow and jerked her arm back. "With force. Give it everything you've got."

The elderly woman copied her move, jabbing backwards with her elbow. "*Ja*, I have it now, Anya," she said, with a satisfied laugh.

"Good job." Anya smiled back at her, pleased she was showing progress, then she moved on to the next person in line. "Ready, Magda?"

"Ready." Magda nodded and then proceeded to show what she could do.

Anya's class was smaller this Sunday evening, with only eight of the ladies showing up. Normally, she would have at least twelve, and when it was a full house, fifteen. Tonight was different because 'The Three Tenors' would be performing in Bremen that evening and quite a few of her students were huge fans. Anya didn't mind, though. A couple of the really talkative ones were among the absentees which meant she would get her students to focus better. There was nothing so distracting as a proud grandmother pulling out photos of the newest addition to the family.

By the end of her volunteer session with her seniors' group, Anya was feeling good. They'd had a productive evening and were all tired, but in a good way. One by one the ladies bid her goodbye and as they filed out, she waved to them then, still smiling, she turned to gather up her things.

The smile froze on her face. Through the plate glass window she saw the figure of a man walking up the pathway and although the shadows of evening had already fallen she knew exactly who that man was. It was Rafe.

What in heaven's name was he doing here? Hadn't she told his friend she had no desire to speak with him? Had Rafe simply ignored what she'd said?

Intent on getting out of there before he entered the building, Anya grabbed her jacket and her shoulder bag, but just as she turned to go, a figure appeared at the door.

"Oh, Anya, I just remembered something." Magda was shaking her head as she walked back into the room. "This is what happens to you when you get old. You forget things all the time."

"Yes, Magda. What is it?" Anya didn't want to sound impatient, but she did want Magda out of there within the next few seconds. As she spoke, she was throwing on her jacket and sliding the strap of her bag onto her shoulder, hopefully making it obvious that she needed to go.

Apparently, it wasn't obvious to Magda because, instead of quickly getting to the point, the woman walked over to one of the benches and took a seat. Then, with no sense of haste at all, she set her big handbag on her knee and began digging through it. "Now let's see," she mumbled. "Where did I put that thing?" She dug some more with Anya standing there, seething the whole time. Of course, Magda didn't notice. "Ah, here it is." She finally pulled out the prize she'd been searching for and held it up with a triumphant grin. "Got it!"

In her hand was a brochure of some sort. As soon as she saw it, Anya's spirit sank. If that brochure was what she thought it was, there went her plan to disappear before Rafe got there. Magda had been planning to take a vacation for ages and she'd said she was going to ask Anya's opinion once she'd narrowed down her choices. She wasn't planning on going through travel brochures right now, was she?

"Magda, can we do this another..." The words were hardly out of her mouth before another shadow appeared in the doorway, this time a tall, lean figure that, despite herself, made her heart thump.

Before she could move, he was walking into the room and, as if all was peachy between them, he was smiling. "Anya," he said, as he came close, "I'm glad I caught you. I didn't realize the car was on empty until

I hopped in. Then there was a line-up at the gas station. Thanks for waiting."

Really? She'd told him not to come, that she didn't want to see him, but he'd come anyway. And now he was thanking her for waiting for him? What kind of game was he playing?

Anya shook her head. "You don't get it, do you? I don't-"

"You sneaky girl. Have you been hiding this young man all this time?" Magda's exultant crow cut her off mid-sentence. "But how could I blame you? This is a handsome one you have here. A real looker." Then, to Anya's surprise, she gave Rafe a look that could only be described as a leer. The woman was something else.

Rafe, on the other hand, was staring at the elderly lady with a look of confusion. Anya knew he spoke some German, but Magda's chatter was like bullets shot from a gun. He looked like he didn't understand a word of her fast talk. And maybe that was a good thing.

"We can talk about my vacation some other time," Magda continued. "It's still a few months away, so no rush. I'll just leave you two love birds alone." She gave Rafe a knowing smile even as she tucked her brochure back into her cavernous handbag. "Good choice, Anya," she said, as her smile widened. "He looks strong. Remember what we told you. Lots and lots of babies." And then, with a satisfied grin, she got up, gave Rafe a friendly nod, and walked out of the room.

Rafe stared after her then turned back to Anya, a slight smile on his lips. "What was that all about?" he asked. "What was she saying about babies?"

Of course, he would have caught that part. Anya shook her head. "It's nothing," she said. "Nothing important, anyway." Then, just in case he'd gotten the idea that he'd successfully wormed his way back into her life, Anya folded her arms across her chest and let her gaze settle on Rafe, except it wasn't so much a gaze as a glare.

She got straight to the point. "What are you doing here?" she asked, her voice devoid of any warmth. "Didn't I tell you I didn't want to see you again?"

Like she'd doused him with ice water, Rafe's brows shot up, and immediately his smile vanished. "What did you say?" His voice came out in a strained whisper, like he was in shock.

She shook her head in disbelief. What kind of game was he really playing? "You heard me," she said, her tone dismissive. "I made it very clear to Khalil that I did not wish to see you and that I would not appreciate your tracking me down. So why are you here? Don't you take no for an answer?"

By this time, the shock was gone from Rafe's face, and in its place was a look of pure anger. His brows drawn, he looked like he would gladly strangle anyone who crossed his path right at that moment.

And that made Anya even more furious. So, he thought he could intimidate her into going out with him? Obviously, he didn't know who he was dealing with.

He took a step forward and made a move like he was raising his hand. "This is crap. Look, Anya, this is all a-"

By this time, he was close enough and, seeing the perfect chance, Anya grabbed his hand and dragged him forward, pitching him off balance. Quick as a flash, she pulled his arm down, twisted it behind his back and shoved it up high, up between his shoulder blades, immobilizing him before he even knew what was happening.

"What the blazes!"

The words ripped from his lips, but by that time, she'd planted the sole of her sneaker squarely in the middle of his back. He was bigger than she was, but she'd caught him off guard, and she planned to use that advantage to the fullest.

Using all the strength of her leg, she gave him a mighty push, making him stagger forward. She didn't even stop to see if he would fall. Like lightning, she was through the door and off down the hallway, not stopping until she'd jumped into her car, gunned the engine and hit the road.

She couldn't believe it. Rafe Kent had shown up at the center even though she'd told him not to. Then, even worse, he'd raised his hand to...hit her? She still couldn't believe it. From the little she knew of Rafe, she would never have thought he would be the type to hit a woman. Had she been that wrong?

Anya gripped the steering wheel even tighter as she stared at the road ahead. Thank goodness she'd been able to protect herself. Her self-defense training had definitely paid off. The act might have been totally uncharacteristic for her, but it had been necessary. No matter how handsome or charming, she'd been taught to defend herself against any man.

Later, the adrenaline pumping in her veins slowed somewhat. And even as she drove, her thoughts thrashing around in her head, she had the presence of mind to realize that it wasn't her body that needed protecting. It was her heart.

And as much as it hurt, she knew that the best thing that could ever happen was for her to never see Rafe Kent again.

CHAPTER SIX

RAFE COULD NOT BELIEVE it. What the hell just happened? One second he was talking to Anya, explaining that Khalil had lied and tricked him into going to see her, and the next, she'd pounced on him, twisted his arm behind his back, then kicked him, almost making him fall flat on his face.

How easily she'd tricked him. At the thought, he grimaced. He, a grown man, caught off guard by a mere slip of a girl. He would have to keep this one to himself or he would be the laughingstock of his friends.

And speaking of friends...with a friend like Khalil, he definitely didn't need enemies. After assuring him everything was arranged, that s0-called friend had sent him here to seek out a woman who didn't even want to see him. In fact, she'd been adamant that she'd told Khalil he should stay away. And still, the guy had let him come looking for her, like some darned fool. Nostrils flaring, Rafe clenched his fists. He was looking forward to breaking Khalil's scrawny neck.

It was a deflated Rafe who climbed into his car and headed back to his motel. It wasn't just that he hadn't gotten the chance to talk to Anya, to let her see that he wasn't the rake his friends had made him out to be. Now, there was another, even more serious, problem. The woman had torn out of the room like she'd just been under attack. From him. He had no doubt that Anya Petersen was now under the distinct impression that he was a stalker of the worst kind.

As he drove, Rafe shook his head. Jesus, what a situation. In all his years dealing with women, this was the first time he'd ever had one flee from him. And it was all the fault of someone he'd called a friend. He would kill him.

But when Rafe got back, marched to Khalil's room and pounded on the door, there was no answer. When he checked back an hour later, there was still no response. Lion was nowhere to be found either, and that was clear evidence that he was party to this whole thing. And, as expected, they'd turned off their cell phones.

Itching to get even, Rafe was so wired, he didn't get to sleep until almost one in the morning. After two more tries that night, he'd finally given up hope of getting his hands on them. It would just have to wait till morning.

By morning, though, it was like the high-tension wire inside him had gone dead. He wasn't even angry anymore. All he felt was drained. He didn't bother to go looking for the guys. In fact, he didn't need to. They came looking for him.

As if they'd done nothing wrong, the two of them stood in his doorway, practically beaming.

"So, how did it go?" Lion asked, his wide grin threatening to split his face in two. "Did you guys kiss and make up?"

Khalil's smile was smug. "I bet they did a whole lot more than that. Our guy looks like he was up all night." Then, he laughed and winked at Lion. "I told you my strategy would work. Just get them together and they'll fall into each other's arms. It's the chemistry between them. Impossible to fight it. Right, Rafe?" He was still chuckling as he raised a hand to touch fists with Rafe.

He didn't get the response he'd expected. Instead of returning the fist bump, Rafe lifted his hand to grab a fistful of Khalil's shirt and drag him into the room. "Don't you ever," he said through clenched teeth, "do that to me again." Then he shoved him away, making Khalil stumble back, his eyes wide with surprise.

"Hey, what did I do?" Rafe's victim asked, his voice breathless. "You're cursing me out for doing you a favor?"

"Favor?" Rafe snarled. "You call that a favor? After assuring me you'd do no such thing, you set me up. Anya didn't agree for me to come. She said she told you she didn't want to see me."

Khalil straightened his shirt then glanced at Lion as if for support. "I never told Rafe she'd agreed to meet with him, did I? I said she was expecting him." He turned back to Rafe. "That's different."

Rafe gave a hiss of annoyance and waved him off. "Semantics. You lied through your teeth, and you know it."

"For a good cause." Lion jumped in. "He was just trying to get you kids back together. He was trying to fix what I'd messed up." He shrugged. "I guess that backfired. Big time." He gave his defender a rueful smile. "Sorry, Khalil."

Rafe had heard enough. He walked over to the bed and flung himself onto it, on his back, then covered his eyes with his arm. "Get out of here, you two," he growled. "I should whup both of you, but right now I'm too tired. Probably wouldn't be worth the trouble, anyway. The damage is already done."

For a long while, there was silence, until Rafe began to wonder if his friends had sneaked out of the room. Then he heard Lion's voice.

"Seriously, Rafe, what happened between you two? It couldn't have been that bad."

How was he supposed to answer that? Rafe grimaced and then he sighed. "Yes, it was that bad. Anya kicked my butt."

"What's that supposed to mean?" This time the question came from Khalil.

Rafe sighed again then lowered his arm so he could see the expressions on his friends' faces when he told them what happened. Right now, he was being a real sucker for punishment. "I went to the center, like you guys told me to do, and I hardly got a sentence out before Anya blasted me, asking me what I was doing there. She wanted to know why I'd come when she'd told me not to." His lips twisted in disgust. "Of course, nobody bothered to tell me that part."

Khalil, the little jerk, shoved his hands in his pockets, but said nothing.

Rafe gave him a cutting look, then he continued. "I tried to explain that I had no idea she'd said that. The next thing I knew, she'd grabbed my arm and twisted it behind my back. Then, she almost broke my back with a hell of a kick." He shook his head. "You could have knocked me over with a feather. Where the heck did that girl learn to fight like that?"

"Oh, yeah. About that." Khalil gave him a guilty look. "I forgot to tell you. The class she was teaching at the center was self defense for seniors. She's got a blue belt in karate."

"You forgot to tell me?"

Khalil shrugged. "I didn't think it was that important."

"Well, it was." Rafe swung his legs off the bed and got up with a sigh of resignation. "But maybe not so much now. After all the damage you guys did, there's no way I'll ever have another chance with Anya. I give up." He headed toward the bathroom. "In fact, I think I'll just call it a day with this whole Europe trek bit. I've had enough."

That got an explosion of reaction from his friends. "What?" The word shot out of Lion's mouth. "You're going to leave us?"

"We've got two more weeks to complete this trip," Khalil said, sounding almost as distressed. "We haven't even hit Austria yet. You can't do this."

Rafe turned and folded his arms across his chest. "Oh, can't I? Want to watch me?"

"Okay, okay, you can," Khalil conceded. "But why pull out early? Since when did Rafe Kent abandon his buddies for some girl?"

"Don't you..." Rafe stopped himself, clamping his mouth shut before he embarrassed himself. He'd been about to say, don't you see, this isn't just some girl. But then, that would draw more questions, and how would he explain? He couldn't even figure out how to explain it to himself. How was it possible that in such a short time Anya had such a hold over him?

He shook his head. "Sorry, guys. I'll have to wrap this up early. Time for me to get my head out of the clouds and back to work." Then, not waiting to see if they'd left or stayed, he walked into the bathroom and closed the door behind him.

And with the closing of that door, he knew another door had closed, too. He would be leaving Europe, relegating that journey to his store of enjoyable recollections, and from here on, Anya Petersen would be nothing but a pleasant memory.

.. ❦ ..

ANYA COULDN'T BELIEVE it was summer break already. Where had the school year gone? Most of the teachers had been dying to start summer vacation, but not her. Her life was so full when she was with the little ones that she didn't have a moment to feel bored. Now, though, they were all off on holidays, so she would be left to her own devices.

It wasn't that she didn't need the rest. When it was work time, she gave it her all, so a vacation was perfectly in order. She deserved it. The only problem was, now that classes had ended, she would have no excuse for putting off a visit to her father in Bonn. A neurologist, he had been sorely disappointed when Anya refused to follow in his footsteps and chose instead to teach at the kindergarten level. She'd had excellent grades in the sciences, acing biology, chemistry and physics. Both of her parents had assumed she would have gone on to study medicine, or at least embark on a career in the science field, but none of that had appealed to Anya. In the end, she had chosen to do what she enjoyed most – working with young children. She loved being a teacher, which gave her the opportunity to mold young minds. She would not have given that up for anything.

And that was why it was so hard for her to spend time with her father. With the coming of the summer vacation, he would expect a visit. Of course, he would use the opportunity to demand to know when she was going to get serious about utilizing her innate acumen for science. In short, he would harass the life out of her.

Her mother, who was also in the medical field, wasn't quite so bad. An obstetrician, she'd been happy when Anya excelled in the sciences, but when her daughter chose to teach children rather than treat them, she'd finally accepted that choice. As she put it so eloquently, you're the one who's going to wake up to this every day. Make sure you don't hate it when Monday morning comes around. Her mother got it, so why didn't her father?

Anya heaved a sigh, then pressed the remote to switch off the television. She'd had enough of *Tatort* for one evening. It was still early yet, only a little after eight o'clock, but she would head for her bedroom, anyway. For some reason, she felt like making it an early night.

Maybe she felt extra tired because, although it was only the first week of summer vacation, she was already bored. Or maybe it was because she'd been thinking about her father and what excuse she could give him for wanting to stay with him only one weekend. Or maybe...maybe it was because, no matter how hard she tried, she could not get a certain man out of her mind, a dark, handsome American by the name of Rafe Kent.

What had the man done to her? Over three weeks had passed since she'd practically assaulted him, then fled out of the building and out of his life, and yet here she was, still thinking about him. This was insane.

Frustrated with how stupid she was being, Anya shook her head in disgust, and got up. She was on her way to the bedroom, when a knock at the door made her halt. She frowned. She wasn't expecting anyone, certainly not at this time of the evening. As she turned to head toward the front door,, the knocking started again and this time it sounded more urgent. "Coming," she called out, and as she reached out to grasp the doorknob, she heard the unmistakable sound of a sob.

Quickly, she opened the door, and as she guessed, it was Helga who stood on her porch, tears streaming down her cheeks.

"May I come in?" the sobbing woman asked. "I can't take it anymore."

"*Mein Gott*. Helga, what did he do this time?" Quickly, Anya skimmed her face, but there were no signs of bruises. She reached out and took her neighbor's hand. "Come in. Tell me what happened."

As she opened the door wide and pulled her inside,, Anya peered through the shadows of dusk across the street to the house that faced hers. *Herr* Gruber was nowhere in sight.

As soon as Helga stepped in, she closed the door and directed the sobbing woman to the long, low sofa in the living room, then sat down beside her. For a long while, Helga didn't speak, and, understanding her distraught state, Anya didn't press her. It took a full minute or more before she stopped twisting her hands on her lap, drew in a deep breath then raised her head. "I'm sorry," she said, her voice breaking. "I didn't want to bother you but I couldn't stay in the house with him another minute."

"It's no bother," Anya said, quick to reassure her. The last thing she wanted was for Helga to feel guilty for seeking help. "You did the right thing. Sometimes, the best thing to do to defuse an argument is to walk away."

"But that's the thing," Helga said, her eyes confused. "We weren't even arguing. He just came home, his face dark as midnight, and started shouting at me. For no reason." She shook her head, almost in a helpless gesture. "It's not like I provoked him or anything."

"Had he been drinking?" Anya asked. "Did he smell like it?"

Again, Helga shook her head. "Not this time. It looks like he came home straight from the office. I don't know what could have made him so angry," she gave a hiccup, "with me. I didn't do anything." Her face crumpled again, and fresh tears began to flow.

"Did he threaten you?" Anya asked. Helga had had run to her for refuge before, but this time, she seemed even more distressed than usual. "Did he hurt you?"

Helga didn't speak. She couldn't. Not with the way her shoulders were shaking, and her lips were trembling. Instead, she put her hand to her lips and nodded.

Anya's brows fell. "He hit you?"

Again, the agitated woman nodded. "And...and this time, I was really scared. It wasn't like before." She dropped her eyes and looked away. "This time," she whispered, "he looked like he wanted to kill me."

That did it for Anya. Immediately, she got up. "Come, Helga. We're going to the police. Right now."

Helga's head jerked up and she stared at Anya, eyes wide. "But that will make him furious."

"You can't help that," Anya said, her voice firm. "What you can do is put a stop to this. You've got to protect yourself. You can't live like this. Now, come." She held out her hands, and when Helga took them, she pulled her neighbor to her feet. "This time you're going to make a formal report to the police," she said, giving the trembling hands a reassuring squeeze. "I'll take you there myself."

At those words, Helga bit her lip, but she was nodding. She was doing the right thing. After months of abuse, it looked like she'd finally found the courage to stand up for herself.

That evening as Anya drove Helga into town, it was as if that gesture of support boosted her confidence, because the flood gates opened and she began to spill so many secrets she'd kept hidden all that time. It was then, that Anya realized that Helga hadn't been suffering for months. The abuse had been going on for over two years, soon after she'd married Karl. The poor woman had been living in hell almost all her married life.

Later, as Helga gave her report to the kind-faced police officer, Anya sat by her side and held her hand. When Helga squeezed her hand and gave her a brave little smile, Anya knew she'd done the right thing in pressing her to make the report. It was a big step for her neighbor, and it was a step in the right direction.

"Tonight, you'll stay with me," Anya said, and when Helga began to shake her head as if in protest, she held up her hand. "No, I insist. The restraining order is being prepared. You will not go back into that house until he's out of there. Think of your safety."

It was those words that made Helga heave a resigned sigh. "You're right," she said quietly. "I've got to stop being so stupid. Karl doesn't love me anymore. I've got to stop thinking about him and start looking out for myself."

Anya didn't respond to that. She'd been saying the same thing to Helga for ages. It had taken a perceived threat against her life to make her take things seriously. Well, better late than never.

When they made their way back home and she parked the car, it was already way past Anya's regular nine o'clock bedtime. She was an early-to-bed, early-to-rise girl who was up hours before sunrise. She didn't mind the disruption to her routine, though. That was an insignificant price to pay to help someone in need.

She hopped out of the car and ran around to the passenger's side to help Helga out.

And that was when she saw him. Lean and wiry, his face was half hidden in shadows, but there was an unmistakable sneer on his lips. Slowly, deliberately, he lifted a cigarette to his lips, but his eyes never left her face.

Although Karl Gruber was on the other side of the street, the menace in his eyes was unmistakable. The dark scowl on his face was clear testament to his rage, but this time it was not directed at his wife. He didn't even spare her a glance.

This time, the target of his fury was Anya herself.

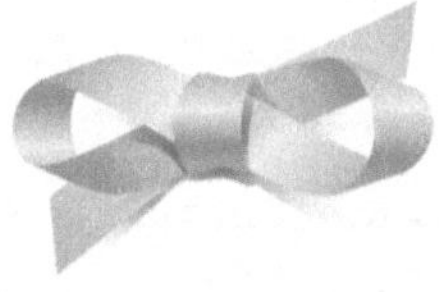

CHAPTER SEVEN

"WHAT ARE YOU GUYS DOING here?" Rafe growled, as he walked out onto the back patio. "I thought Ransom and Solie were doing this barbecue in my honor. Just me."

Ridge laughed and walked over to slap his younger brother on the back. "Sorry to disillusion you. The only reason you were invited is that they need somebody to do the dishes afterwards. Now come here, you runt. Long time no see." His words were followed by a bone-crushing bear hug.

Rafe groaned. He should have known better. There was no way Ransom would do a barbecue and not have all brothers present. Ryder, the third in the family, he didn't mind. But Ridge? With the family troublemaker present, there was no telling what could go down.

When Ridge finally released him, he stepped back, flexed his shoulders and grimaced. "Still working out in the gym, I see. You didn't have to take it out on me, though."

"Stop being such a wimp." Ridge only laughed and gave him another hearty slap on the shoulder, almost dislocating it. It didn't help that his older brother, at six feet four inches, was even taller than he was, and big and brawny to boot. The man didn't know his own strength. "Those weeks you spent in Europe turned you soft, kiddo?"

"Far from it." They both turned to see Ransom, the oldest brother in the clan, stepping out the back door. He had a crooked grin on his lips. "From what I heard ,our kid brother was anything but soft as he went from city to city. Seems he left lots of lonely ladies in his wake."

Rafe's eyes narrowed as he turned to face his brother. "Where did you hear that?"

Ransom shrugged. "Let's just say, I have my sources."

That made Rafe snort, as he shoved his hands in his pockets and turned away from Ransom's mocking grin. He didn't have to think long and hard to figure out the 'source'. His friends weren't strangers to his family, and keeping secrets had never been Lion's strong point. He'd learned his lesson. At all costs, keep his friends and his family as far away as possible.

"Heard you had a renegade employee. How're you handling that?" It was Ryder, the quiet one, who was now taking charge of the conversation. You could always trust him to get serious. As he sat lounging in the wicker patio chair, a bottle of Heineken beer in his hand, he looked relaxed, but alert, and all business. Typical Ryder, he'd never been one to just relax and forget about work for a while.

"Things are cool," Rafe said, his tone nonchalant. "As soon as I got back, I got rid of him. I've got a new guy in his position now."

"Headhunter helped you out?" Ryder asked. "Take you long to find him?"

"Nope and nope. I just promoted one from within the ranks. The whistle blower."

Ryder cocked his head to one side as he stared back at Rafe. "Sure that was the best move?"

"What if this guy set the first one up?" Ransom asked, as he grabbed a beer from the cooler. "What if he had an ulterior motive?"

"Yeah, lil bro," Ridge cut in. "What if that was his plan all along? He could have been in on things all this time, and then let the guy take the fall so he could muscle his way in, take over as the man in charge. Get what I'm saying?"

"I get you, but I checked him out, too. He's clean." Rafe shook his head. "Give me some credit, guys. I'm not as dumb as I look."

Ridge gave a grunt. "You could've fooled me."

Ridge was expert at needling you till you were forced to tackle him, but Rafe wasn't falling for that bait this time. As old as he was, there was nothing Ridge liked more than a rough and tumble tackle, but this time he wasn't going to get that satisfaction. If there was one thing Rafe had learned over the years, it was never to take on your brother when he outweighs you by more than forty pounds.

"Long time no see, little brother."

At the sound of the laughing, lilting voice, Rafe turned around to see Solie standing in the doorway, looking as fresh and lovely as usual. Immediately, he smiled, and as he held his arms wide, she walked into them and he hugged her tight. Then, he set her away from him and looked down into her smiling face. "So, how's my favorite sister-in-law?" he asked.

"Oh, stop it," she said, giving him a not-too-gentle punch on the arm. "I'm your only sister-in-law. Come on, you can do better than that."

"Okay, okay," he said, putting his hands up in self defense. "How's my favorite Panamanian girl?"

She frowned. "And how many other Panamanian girls do you know?"

"Okay, how's my favorite nurse?" he threw out quickly, before she got it in her head to punch him again. Solie lifted weights at the gym, and the strength of her punch was testament to its effect.

"Now that, I like," she said with a wide smile. "Now, don't you forget it."

"I won't," he assured her, brows lifted in earnest. He was scared of Solie and her punches, and she knew it.

She laughed and walked over to where her husband stood watching them, his grin making it clear that he was enjoying his wife's bullying of his youngest brother. His brows lifted in surprise, though, when she planted her palm in the middle of his chest and gave him a shove, sending him falling backward to plop his rear on the padded wicker sofa behind him. Then, without ceremony, the petite woman sat, too, making herself comfortable right on his lap.

Rafe could only shake his head and chuckle. It wasn't hard to tell who wore the pants in this house. Ransom had his hands full with this one, which was just as it should be. He was so used to being the oldest, and the one in charge, that it was good to see him bossed around now and again. And this was one of those times.

That evening, Rafe had a good time at Ransom and Solie's. Although he'd complained about his brothers being there, he'd actually been pleased they'd come. They didn't often get a chance to hang out together and catch up, and he knew it was mostly because of him. He'd gathered the reputation of being the family "rolling stone", the one who would look for adventure in the most unlikely places. The thing was, he'd never been a 'suit and tie', in-office kind of guy. In fact, the last few weeks he'd spent at his corporate office, straightening out the latest issue, had been out of character for him. And now, he was restless. And ready to wander.

After the meal, when Solie and Ransom had gone indoors to chill a while in front of the T.V., and Ryder had left for home, Rafe took Ridge into his confidence. Knowing Ridge, notorious as a trickster, that was probably a big mistake, but Rafe decided to take a chance.

"What would you do," he asked Ridge, "if you met a lady who lives thousands of miles away, wants absolutely nothing to do with you but, for the life of you, you can't get her out of your mind?"

"That's easy," Ridge said, with a smirk. "I'd get my private jet, go to her wherever she was, charm the socks off of her, and get her to come back with me. Then, I'd never let her out of the country."

Rafe sighed. "I wish it were as easy as that."

"So, what's up lil bro'? Don't tell me you went to Europe and fell in love." Ridge shook his head. "After Rhonda ditched you, I didn't think you would tie yourself to any other woman. Use them and lose them. That was your motto, right?"

Rafe gave him a cutting glance.

"Sorry," Ridge said, with a grimace. "Didn't mean to throw that in your face." Then, he jerked his chin toward Rafe. "But don't keep me in suspense, dude. What's this all about?"

Rafe got up from the bar stool on which he'd perched and walked to the end of the patio, his back to Ridge. Then, as he tried to figure out how to explain things, he shoved his hands deep inside his pockets.

After a long silence, he spoke. "Her name is Anya," he said, his voice low. "Anya Petersen. From Germany." He cleared his throat. "I met her all of five times, but Christ, I just can't get her out of my mind."

"Uh-huh." Ridge nodded. "One of those, huh?"

With his back still to Ridge, Rafe frowned. "One of those?"

"Damn good in bed. Can't get her out of your system," Ridge said, his voice smug. "I know those kinds of women."

This time, Rafe turned to face his brother, his frown now a glare. "Shut the hell up. It wasn't like that. Not with Anya."

Brows raised, Ridge stared back at him. "Oh? So, what was it like, then? What the heck are you talking about?"

"I'm talking about a woman I admire and respect. Anya is...different. Different from any woman I've ever known."

Ridge looked skeptical. "So, what makes this one so special?"

Rafe didn't have to think twice. "She's smart and funny and super-independent. And, trust me, she knows how to take care of herself." He gave Ridge a rueful grin. "If you're ever looking for a bodyguard, she'd be perfect for the job."

"Meaning?"

"That's another story for another time." Rafe wasn't about to embarrass himself with an account of that episode. "She's one-of-a-kind, Ridge. Once you meet her, you'll know what I mean."

"Once I meet her?" Ridge cocked an eyebrow. "You talk as if you're serious about this girl. She must really be something."

"She is." Slowly, Rafe nodded. "And that's why, some way, somehow, I've got to see her again." Then, he sighed. "Even though she doesn't want to see me."

Ridge's frown deepened and that was when Rafe realized, if he was asking his brother's advice, he would have to give him the full story. So, he did; every last word of it, even the part about almost tumbling face first to the floor, compliments of little Miss Petersen.

"Sounds like a real special girl," Ridge said, his grin wide. "I like her already."

By the time they'd finished discussing his dilemma, Rafe had a plan...of sorts. A plan concocted by Ridge. "How the heck am I going to get a position teaching at her school?" Rafe asked. He wasn't liking Ridge's idea too much. What was he going to do? Storm the school? "And what about teaching experience? What kind of operation would hire me without that?"

Instead of an explanation, Ridge gave him a confident smile. "Leave all of that to me," he said, his look enigmatic. "Just get your teacher cap on. School starts early in Germany. You've got two weeks."

• • ❧ • •

"*Guten Morgen, Herr Kent.*" The tiny tots raised their squeaky voices in greeting. Some said the words at the top of their voices, some spoke shyly, while others just mumbled. But they were all staring up at Rafe with rapt attention. And no wonder. At his height, he was towering over this junior kindergarten class.

Trying to make himself less intimidating, Rafe dipped his head and gave the children a friendly smile. "*Guten Morgen, Kinder,*" he replied, as he surveyed the group.

"And now in English, children." Mrs. Rosner gave the children a nod and again they raised their voices in greeting. "Good morning, Mr. Kent."

"Good morning, children."

Then, the greetings over, the children plopped back down onto the circular mat in the middle of the room and reached for the toys and books they'd abandoned when their teacher asked them to stand and greet the new addition to the Coleman Private English School family.

Rafe, standing there in the middle of the room, was way out of his depth. There was no denying that. In fact, right then, he was wondering how he could have been such a fool to listen to Ridge. What an ass he was, following a plan cooked up by the one brother he knew was not to be trusted. For all he knew, Ridge had come up with this idea to embarrass the heck out of him. He wasn't called the family prankster for nothing.

But now was not the time to be having second thoughts, not when he was already in Germany, starting his first day at the school where Anya worked, standing in front of his very own class. Well, it wasn't exactly his class. Rafe had been assigned as an intern to Mrs. Rosner's class, a student teacher in need of work experience. And it had all been set up by Ridge.

"There's hardly anything in this world," Ridge had told him, "that money can't buy."

Apparently, he'd been right. Before Rafe knew what was up, Ridge was telling him that everything had been arranged. A hefty donation to the school had convinced the founder and principal to take the benefactor's younger brother on board to allow him to gain some teaching experience. She'd even overlooked the fact that his experience was in the corporate world and not in the education field. Ridge had only asked for three months, so she probably thought it was a small price to pay for the security of a monetary gift that could keep her entire teaching staff employed for a year. Who knew what lay behind that lady's ultimate decision? Rafe only hoped that despite his misgivings, all of this would make things work out in his favor.

But now, to deal with the task at hand – how to relate to a classroom full of three and four year olds - still nothing but babies, as far as he was concerned - when you knew absolutely nothing about working with young children.

"Come, Mr. Kent, you may sit here." Mrs. Rosner directed him to the floor, to a spot right between a dark-haired boy and a tiny girl who stared up at him, eyes big as saucers.

Rafe glanced at his supervisor. "Are you sure?" he whispered. "I don't want to scare them."

Shaking her head, she smiled. "They'll be fine," she said gently. "I have a feeling you're more afraid than they are." She held out her hand again, pointing to the spot between the two children. "Now, come. Sit. It's time for us to sing our happy morning song."

And that was how Rafe ended up on the floor, long legs stretched out before him, feeling like a giant among a throng of elves. He was the only big one there. Even Mrs. Rosner was small, not even five feet tall, with a cherubic face that made her look like one of the children, even though she was old enough to be Rafe's mother. Great. Just what he needed, to not only feel stupid and out-of-place, but to look stupid and out-of-place as well.

Feeling like a perfect dork, Rafe sang the ABC song and 'The Wheel on the Bus', doing the hand movements and everything. Thank God no-one he knew was seeing him like that. He would never live that down.

He gave a soft sigh of relief when it was time to break for the mid-morning snack. There was just so much smiling, singing and wiping little runny noses that he could take for one morning. Eager to split, he got up and turned toward the door.

"Where are you going?" Claire Rosner's voice brought him to a halt.

"Uh, out?" He turned to give her a quizzical look. "I thought this was time for a break."

The august lady looked at him over her glasses. "No, Mr. Kent. That's not how it works here. We make sure all the children have taken their bathroom breaks and have eaten before we leave this room. Now, would you be so kind as to take the boys to the rest room, please?"

Rafe suppressed a groan. He should have known this job wasn't going to be easy. The things a man had to do to get close to a woman. Jeez.

It was when he got to the bathroom that he realized how helpless the little ones were. There were six of them and he ended up having to help them undress so they could take care of business, then he had to lift them so they could wash their tiny hands. The fact that they were a rambunctious little bunch didn't make things any easier. While he was helping one child, two of them made a dash for the hallway. In two strides he'd caught the kicking, squirming bundles and brought them to heel, but not before he got a good, solid kick in the gut from one of his struggling captives.

It was a slightly winded Rafe who made his way back to the kindergarten room, six little munchkins in tow. He was only too glad to deposit them in front of their teacher, who immediately took charge, helping them with their lunch bags, and making sure they started with the healthy stuff. It was obvious that the children knew who was in charge. The eight girls were already seated in a neat row, munching on apples, carrots and sandwiches as they watched the boys ready themselves for lunch.

"If you need a quick break," Mrs. Rosner said, as she reached over to open a container for one of the boys, "now is the time. I'll be here with the children."

"Are you sure?" Rafe glanced at the group. Although they were quiet, he knew that if they became restless, they could be quite the handful.

The woman smiled. "I think I'll be able to manage for a few minutes without you. Now go, but be back in fifteen minutes."

"No problem." Rafe nodded. Fifteen minutes was all he needed. He would use the time to run down to the teachers' lounge to try to find

Anya. This was his sole purpose for being at the school and he didn't want to waste another minute. He had to see her, and soon. Like right now.

He'd turned, ready to make his escape, when there was a rap at the door. He kept on moving. He would direct whoever it was to Mrs. Rosner. The visitor would not have come to see him, anyway. He hadn't even been introduced to the rest of the staff yet.

Determined not to be held up for any reason, Rafe flung the door open. The words died on his lips. There, standing in front of him, looking even more beautiful than ever, stood the woman he'd practically changed careers to pursue.

After a wait of over six weeks, he was finally face-to-face with Anya again.

CHAPTER EIGHT

SHOCK COURSED THROUGH Anya as she stared up into the face of the man she'd thought she would never see again. Rafe Kent! What in goodness gracious was he doing at Coleman School?

"Rafe," she gasped, not able to stop herself. "What are you doing here?" Her hand flew up to clutch her scarf in an involuntary gesture of self defense. Had he tracked her down?

"Anya." For some strange reason, Rafe looked surprised, almost as if he hadn't expected to see her. But that didn't make sense at all. Wasn't he the one who had sought her out? That was the only reason he was at the school, wasn't it?

Within a fraction of a second, his look of surprise disappeared, his face softening into a look of pleasure. "I didn't expect to see you at the door," he said. "The principal told you I was here?"

Struck dumb by his remark, Anya could only shake her head. Whatever did he mean?

Before either of them could say another word, Mrs. Rosner broke in. "Anya. I thought you'd forgotten about the art kit. Come in. I'll go and get it for you." As she spoke, she was heading for the cupboard in the corner. "I see you've met my intern. You knew each other before?"

"Your...intern?" Eyes wide, Anya looked from Mrs. Rosner then back to Rafe who had stepped aside to let her in and now stood there, beaming.

"Yes, and he came at the right time, too. Just when I needed someone to take over since Diana left." She turned to Rafe. "Diana was my intern last term. She's all done with her training now."

"Oh. Perfect timing." Rafe nodded, then he chuckled. "Although I was hoping to be assigned to a slightly older group."

Claire laughed. "Instead, you got the babies. But don't you worry. Once you get used to them you'll see they're the easiest group to manage."

He gave her a doubtful look. "I hope so."

As they spoke, Anya could not help staring at one, then the other. What in the world was going on? Since when did the school start hiring strangers off the street? Last time she'd seen Rafe almost two months before, he'd been nothing but a tourist wandering through Europe, clad in denim shirt and khaki trousers, sporting a ponytail.

She had to admit, though, that now he looked like a perfect gentleman in his pleated navy-blue trousers, long-sleeved shirt and conservative tie. And, to her surprise, the ponytail was gone. And even as she gazed at him, looking so different in his professional attire, memories came flooding back and she knew he was the same charming foreigner she'd fallen in love with.

At that thought, Anya dropped her gaze. Fallen in love? A bit too strong, maybe. All right, a lot too strong. How could she have fallen in love with someone she'd only met a few times, someone she'd thought she would never see ever again?

But whether it made sense or not, there it was. The erratic heartbeats, the heat rising in her face, the suddenly sweaty palms, the feeling like she was having trouble breathing. And this wasn't a panic attack. How could it be, when even as her body gave this violent response to his presence, her heart was melting into a mushy mess of pleasure. No matter that her brain was trying to rebel against the very idea, there was no denying the fact that she was glad to see him.

But that was beside the point. She had to get out of there. Fast. This man was dangerous, in more ways than one.

"Here you go."

Before the words were properly out of her colleague's mouth, Anya stepped past Rafe to grab the box of art supplies. "Thanks, Claire," she said, her voice distressingly breathless. "I'll get it back to you by the end of the week."

"No rush, my dear." The older lady dismissed her with a wave of the hand. "I have a spare one I can use if I need anything."

"Okay, thank you." Anya turned, deliberately keeping her eyes downcast so she wouldn't have to see those amber eyes staring back at her. Then, just so Claire didn't think she was being strange, she gave Rafe a brusque farewell nod then fled, not stopping till she was safely back inside her classroom. Thank goodness her class of five-year olds had already gone out to the playground with her assistant. The sight of their teacher dashing, panting into the room and slamming the door shut behind her, would not have gone down well at all.

Anya staggered away from the door and over to her desk where she plopped down into her chair, still shaking from the shock of seeing Rafe again. How in the world could this have happened? Rafe and her in the same workplace? What were the odds of something like that happening? She shook her head. No, this was no coincidence. The first chance she got she would speak to the principal. She had to get to the bottom of this.

But Anya never got the chance. Not that day, anyway. At the clanging of the last bell, she helped her group gather their belongings and escorted them out to the parking area where the school buses and parents were waiting. As soon as the last child was collected, she ran back to the office, intent on seeking audience with her boss.

Too late. There, in the main office, stood Rafe. His back was to her. He was speaking with the receptionist, and it looked like he was doing an excellent job of charming the socks off the woman, mature though she was. Whatever he was saying to her must have been tremendously intriguing because she seemed totally entranced.

Anya's brows fell. For a man like Rafe, it was too easy. Had she been charmed just as easily?

Swiftly, she turned, planning to disappear before he even realized she'd entered the room. But then, as if alerted by some sort of signal, he looked up, and his leonine eyes locked with hers.

Immediately, he smiled. "Anya. I'm glad I caught you. I thought you'd already left." And, just like that, he began walking toward her, acting like they were old friends. When he was standing right in front of her, he cocked his head to one side. "Do you have a minute?" he asked. "Can we talk?"

As she gazed up at him, alarm bells went off in Anya's head. Tell him no, they warned. That's the last thing you want to do. Stay away from this man. But the pounding of her heart was drowning out the bells, and as she opened her mouth, she knew she was going to say yes.

But then, she blinked, and that was what brought her back to her senses. "Um, no," she said, her voice low so no-one else could hear. "We have nothing to talk about."
And before he could stop her, she turned on her heels, and hurried out the door.

. . ⚭ . .

THAT AFTERNOON WHEN Rafe walked into the apartment he'd rented, he slammed the door shut behind him. Was this how it was going to be? He'd traveled all the way to Germany, committed himself to a three-month stint working in an area he knew nothing about, just for a chance to be close to Anya again...only to have her slam that door right in his face. He was the biggest fool in the world, that was for sure. He should never have listened to Ridge and his harebrained schemes. He could just imagine his brother's reaction when he told him how things had worked out. Ridge would laugh him from here to kingdom come. Sympathy had never been one of his strong points.

Feeling deflated, Rafe didn't even bother to get his frozen dinner from the refrigerator. Food was the farthest thing from his mind. Right then, what he needed was distraction. He flung himself down onto the sofa, reached for the remote-control device, and clicked on the television.

He'd been flipping channels for all of seven minutes before he groaned, ready to give up. Over a hundred channels, and not a damn thing to watch. A lot of the channels were in German, and he just wasn't in the mood to follow fast-talking native German speakers just then. Other channels were in French, Spanish and Italian and the few English channels he could find were boring as heck. So much for finding his distraction on T.V.

He was just about ready to give up, when he switched to a station that was clearly a religious one. The group of young people sitting on a grassy hill were singing a hymn that was known worldwide. "Amazing Grace," they sang. "How sweet the sound."

Although it wasn't his usual cup of tea, it sounded pretty good, kind of soothing to his restless spirit, and Rafe settled back in the seat to enjoy the song. As soon as they were done, he reached for the remote, ready to move on to something with a bit more excitement, but just as he was about to press the button, something on the screen caught his eye, and he frowned. No, not something. Someone.

Eyes narrowed, he stared at the youngster seated in the back row, his round face beaming as he sang. Rafe frowned. He knew that face. For the life of him, he couldn't say from where, but he just knew that he knew him.

And then, the kid got up from the grassy bank and walked to the front then turned to face the group. "Thank you, everyone," he said, in a voice that was surprisingly big and bold. "That was wonderful singing, a great start to our meeting."

It was when he heard the voice that Rafe realized who it was. The kid. Carlos. The one who had joined in the pillow fight and almost murdered him with pillow pounding. Carlos, who had come to Germany to set up a church, was now featured on one of the local religious channels. The kid hadn't been lying, after all.

His interest in the program renewed, Rafe settled back to watch, and that was how he learned about all the work that Carlos and his group were doing in the tiny town of Rothenberg. They'd set up a soup kitchen which did daily food distribution to the less fortunate in their community. They'd helped to build two homes after acquiring donations of two plots of land. Now, they were trying to raise funds to acquire a third. Last on their list, they wanted to build a church.

"This is not an easy task," Carlos told them. "I know it is easy to get discouraged, especially when the need is so great and our resources are so small. Still, we have to keep going. We cannot stop trying, not when there are people in dire need. I implore you, never give up."

That drew some nods and a few claps, but Rafe could see the looks of concern on many of the faces. Carlos, though, did not seem deterred. His message was about hope and faith, and by the end of the sermon, there was a visible change in the group. Their faces brighter now, the people nodded with each new point that Carlos made.

"I believe in miracles," he declared. "Miracles come from unexpected places. We may have dreams, dreams to be an uplifting force, and those dreams may be challenged. But we should never despair, not when the Lord is on our side."

Rafe would never have guessed it, not when he'd met the unassuming kid in the hostel room, but Carlos was a great motivational speaker. He could see that now. When he'd wrapped up his message and the group began to sing again, there was not one face on the T.V. screen that didn't have a wide smile.

Rafe continued watching until the credits began floating up the screen. Hope United. That was what the group was called. And they were only a few hundred miles away. He knew exactly where to look if he wanted to find Carlos.

And Rafe decided he would do just that. He'd been down in the dumps, feeling dejected at the thought of a girl who wouldn't even give him the time of day, but then his consciousness had been jarred by a humble fellow who had dedicated his life to helping others. Carlos had spoken about his lofty goals to do a whole lot more in the community. He'd also made it clear that they were far from achieving the financial goals that would help them realize that dream. Still, he admonished his team not to get discouraged because, as he put it, he believed in miracles.

"Well, Carlos," Rafe muttered to himself, smiling as he scribbled down the name of the church, "say hello to your next miracle." His smile widening into a self-satisfied grin, he got up and went to pick up his phone off the kitchen counter where he'd dropped it. He dialed the number to his office.

"Sarah," he said, as soon as his director of diversity and donations answered her phone, "I have the perfect project for you. It's a bit outside of our usual focus, but I think it's worth adding to our list."

But when Rafe gave her the details, she was less than enthused. "We don't do religious organizations," she said drily. "You know that, Rafe. That could get us in trouble, even though we might mean well. We don't want to get tied to any religious group. You know that could backfire."

"So, okay, they're a religious group. So what? They're just like any of the other charities we support."

"No, they're not." Sarah's tone was adamant. "You give to one religious group, then we get branded as Catholic, Baptist or some other thing we're not. I don't want to go there."

But Rafe wasn't taking no for an answer. In the end, the buck would stop right at his feet, and he was prepared to deal with the repercussions if and when they ever came. "So, donate to ten different religious organizations then. That way we can't be tied to any particular one. That's part of what I hired you for, isn't it? Diversity. Now, go make it work."

Sarah gave an audible groan. "This could come back to bite you, Rafe. But, if you insist…"

"I insist," he replied. "I feel strongly about this one, Sarah. They're making a difference in their community. We can help them do that. Now, get cracking."

She sighed. "All right."

"And Sarah?"

"Yes, sir?" When she addressed him like that, Rafe knew it meant she was not happy. Too bad. He was not about to change his mind because of her misgivings.

"Make sure it's anonymous."

"Of course, sir." She grated out the last word.

Rafe didn't give a hoot. When he clicked the phone off, he was smiling. His mood had moved up ten notches in the space of ten minutes. Even though he'd never carried himself like a man with money, now it felt darned good to be rich. He'd been able to work a well-needed miracle with one simple phone call. And, like he'd always known, the best remedy for a blue mood was to do something good for someone else. It felt good to do good.

And maybe it was because he was in a better mood, but where the thought of Anya's rejection had earlier depressed him, now he was looking at things from a whole new perspective. So, she hadn't welcomed him with open arms. That was understandable. She must have been in shock at the sight of him.

And, just thinking about things, he now knew what he should do. He would back off and give Anya her space. For the rest of the week, he would make no attempt to get her to meet with him. Give her time to get used to the idea that he was around – that was the best thing to do.

After all, he was going to be in Germany a whole three months. That was lots of time for him to work his way back onto her good side.

Because, if he knew anything about women, the one thing guaranteed to get them interested in you was to act like you weren't noticing them at all.

CHAPTER NINE

RAFE KENT WAS BACK in Germany and Anya was scared out of her wits. Not only was he a womanizer, but the last time they'd met, he'd raised his hand in anger, a sign that below the surface he must have a violent temper. No matter how attracted she was to him, he was not the kind of man she wanted in her life. Not now. Not ever.

After what she'd seen Helga go through, she would be a fool to get involved with a man like that. And that was why it was so important for her to stay the heck out of his way.

Under the circumstances, it would be a challenging task. After all, they were now co-workers. There was no way she could avoid him, but what she could do was make sure he would never catch her by herself. That way, he'd never get the chance to make a move on her.

As Anya stripped and stepped into the shower, she heaved a sigh. Why couldn't things be simple and clear-cut? If Rafe had an evil streak, why couldn't he look evil, or at least, not look so awfully delicious he made your mouth water?

After the shock of seeing Rafe, Anyafe lt so emotionally drained, she decided to make it an early night. It was just a little after eight when she crawled into bed then reached over and switched off the lamp. With the room bathed in darkness, she breathed a soft sigh, and sank into the pillows. She had no idea when sleep finally claimed her.

Anya's body was soon lost in slumber. Her mind, though, could not have been busier. She was dreaming, and the subject of her dream was tall and mysterious, his face hidden in shadows. But even as he was shrouded in darkness, there was an aura about this mystery man, one that drew her with the pull of an all-powerful magnet. He was dangerous. She could feel it. The nearer she got, the faster her heart raced, but, try as she might, there was nothing she could do to resist him. She could not get away.

It was when she got close that she saw his eyes, the color of a fiery blaze, translucent and shimmering with the flickering light of a thousand flames. Like he was welcoming her home, he held out his arms, and as he did, she was enveloped in his warmth. Powerless to deny him, she stepped forward, eager to fall into his embrace.

But as she took the first step, she was jerked off her feet. The earth pounded beneath, shuddering and shaking, making her pitch forward and fall to the ground. Even as she clung to the ground, digging her fingers into the dirt, the pounding began again, louder this time, jarring her brain with the violent vibrations of a jackhammer.

"Uh, what?" Anya jerked awake and her eyes flew open, but all she could see was darkness. She sucked in her breath, still shaking from the shock of her nightmare, her pajama top damp and clinging to her skin. Slowly, she exhaled.

"It's only a dream," she muttered. "Only a dream." Then, she drew in another deep breath, trying to steady her nerves.

Where had that nightmare come from? She hadn't had one of those in years. This whole Rafe thing, with him showing up out of the blue, was having a serious effect on her. What was she going to do?

Anya threw back the covers. She was feeling too hot, too sticky, to lie down, and she badly needed a glass of water.

But, just as her toes touched the floor, the silence of the night was shattered by a horrendous hammering. Someone was downstairs pounding on her back door.

Eyes wide, Anya's gaze flew to the digital clock on the nightstand. Three forty-three. Who could be at her door at this hour?

Her heart jerked in fright. It could only mean one thing. There must be a fire!

Heart pounding, she jumped off the bed and ran to the door, then she flipped on the hallway light and flew down the stairs. She was dashing down the hallway toward the back door when she skidded to a halt. She'd thought there was a fire, but where was the smoke? The hallway light partially illuminated the path to the kitchen, but there was no sign of smoke, and it didn't smell like anything was burning. Could she have been mistaken?

A new fear gripped her. Someone was at her door, and she had no idea why.

Her heart beating a staccato rhythm, her breathing quickened by fright, Anya moved into the shadows and crept stealthily toward the back door. She had no intention of opening to anyone. In fact, her first instinct was to call the police, but she had to see who it was. What if it was Helga seeking refuge in the middle of the night?

The kitchen bathed in darkness, Anya sneaked in, glad that she didn't need light to know exactly where everything was. Silently, she slipped over to the curtained window. Making sure she could not be seen, she crouched down by the sill, shifted the curtain ever so slightly, and peered through.

What she saw made Anya suck in a sharp breath. There, on her back porch, stood a shadowy figure, much too tall to be Helga. It was the dark and dangerous man from her dream.

Anya gasped again and made to move back, ready to dash to her room and to safer ground. She would lock herself in and call the police from there. She was pulling back from the window when the man stepped forward, raised his fist and began pounding on the door.

"Come out of there, you damn busybody," he yelled, his German almost incomprehensible. His voice was so slurred it was obvious he was drunk as a sailor. "You turned her against me. It's all your fault." His words broke off on a hiccup then a sob. "You destroyed my life, you bitch!" And then he began beating on her door again, this time longer and louder, banging like he planned to break it down.

Not waiting another second, Anya backed away, then turned and streaked back the way she'd come, through the house and up the stairs, not stopping till she'd slammed her bedroom door behind her. She flipped the lock, and although it was flimsy, it made her feel a tiny bit more secure.

But she didn't stop there. There was no way she was going to have a crazy man banging on her door. What if he got the insane idea to break in?

As she grabbed the phone to call the police, she bit her lip. She'd thought Rafe Kent was the worst of her problems, but now she was facing a threat far more serious. If Karl Gruber was who Helga said he was, that man was the last person anybody would want as their enemy.

. . ✑ . .

WHEN RAFE KENT MADE up his mind to do something, you could consider it good and done. He'd said he was going to give Anya her space, and that was exactly what he'd been doing all week. After the way she'd doused him with cold water that first day, he wasn't giving her a second chance. Not for a while, anyway. Not until he'd given her time to get over whatever her problem was so that she could at least not run, the minute she saw him.

And so, next day when Rafe saw Anya in the teachers' lounge, he gave her the coolest of nods, and later, when the principal called the staff together so that he could be formally introduced, he gave the same polite little smile he gave everyone else.

By Wednesday, when he ran into her in the cafeteria, Anya's glance had changed from surprised and cautious, to openly curious. He could just imagine the questions floating around in her head. Why the sudden change, she must be wondering. How come he's not trying to make conversation? Why is he ignoring me?

Well, he wouldn't be giving her any answers. Only when her curiosity was at its peak would he even consider approaching her again.

Soon, though, there were other matters that effectively distracted Rafe from his interest in Anya. With a class full of little tykes, he had his hands full each day, but by his third day at the school, there was one little boy who really sparked his interest. Little Albert was a shy child, which wasn't so strange for one who was only four years old. But that wasn't what caught Rafe's attention. There was an air of sadness about the little one that made Rafe spend just a little more time playing with him, trying to draw him out of his shell. What could have happened in the life of one so young, to make him afraid to smile? How could a child, hardly more than a baby, resist the urge to run and play?

Unable to suppress his curiosity and concern, Rafe decided to get some answers. "What's Albert's background?" he asked Mrs. Rosner. "Is everything all right at home?"

The lady shook her head. "I have no idea," she said. "Albert just started at our school this year. I'm just getting to know him myself, but I did notice he's a bit on the quiet side." Then, she smiled. "It's good that you're so concerned, but maybe it's nothing but a bit of shyness. I think he'll fit in very soon."

Rafe appreciated that she was trying to reassure him, but he was far from convinced. What he was seeing was no ordinary shyness. When he looked into those soft brown eyes, there was a sadness lingering there that should never be seen in the eyes of a child. "What do you think," he said, speaking slowly as the thought came to him, "if we ask his parents to come in? Maybe if we speak with them, they can shed some light on what's going on with him."

Mrs. Rosner's smile deepened. "I like you. I really do."

That made Rafe give her a confused smile. "Thanks, but what makes you say that?"

"You show great promise as a teacher. I can see that you truly care about your students." She nodded, lending emphasis to her words. "You didn't come into the field of teaching for the money. You're doing this because you care." She slid her glasses off her forehead and back onto her nose. "That's an excellent idea. I'll call and see if I can set up an early meeting with his parents. You're very observant, Rafe. Good job."

True to her word, Rafe's supervisor arranged for the meeting to take place the very next afternoon, but when there was a tap at the door of the small conference room and it opened, it was a single woman, looking very young and very shy, who entered. She looked little more than a teenager, but Rafe assumed she was in her early twenties.

She looked surprised when he got up to greet her. "Welcome Mrs. Kaufmann. Please. Have a seat." He directed her to the chair across from Mrs. Rosner. "May I offer you something to drink? Coffee? Tea?" He waved his hand toward the tea tray they'd set up for the meeting. "What about a glass of water?"

"Oh, no. No, thank you. I'm fine."

She had a hesitant voice, and it was so soft that Rafe was having a hard time hearing her. He couldn't help wondering if he and the lead teacher were so intimidating that they'd made the woman lose her voice. Maybe he was the problem, what with the way he towered over her diminutive frame. Best to get his butt back in his chair so the poor girl wouldn't feel so overwhelmed.

"I'm glad you could come," Mrs. Rosner said, as soon as Rafe had returned to his seat. "We were expecting your husband, too. Couldn't he make it?"

To Rafe's surprise, Mrs. Kaufmann suddenly turned pale, and then her face reddened, and she dropped her gaze. Confused, Rafe looked at his fellow teacher, but the look she gave him told him she was just as confused.

"Is something wrong, *Frau* Kaufmann?" Mrs. Rosner leaned forward. "You're not feeling well?"

"No, I'm...I'm fine." She shook her head, and when she glanced up, her look was apologetic. "I'm sorry. I'm just not...used to it yet."

"Used to it? Used to what, exactly?" Rafe asked the question as gently as he could. The last thing he wanted to do was upset the woman further.

"Used to the idea that...David is gone." The last part was said in a wide-eyed whisper, almost like she was still in shock. "He died...three months ago and...and I still can't believe it."

"*Mein Gott!* I am so sorry." Mrs. Rosner made as if to get up and go to her, but *Frau* Kaufmann held up her hand.

"It's okay. I'll be all right. I just need a moment." She swallowed, then drew in a shaky breath. When she exhaled, she gave them a tremulous smile. "I'm fine now. We can talk. Please. Go ahead."

Doubtful that she was ready as she said she was, Rafe remained silent and sat back in his chair, waiting for Mrs. Rosner to take the lead. As the senior teacher, she would have to be the one to start the discussion.

The lady cleared her throat, seeming somewhat uncertain. Like Rafe, she must have been thrown off by the visitor's sad news. "Thank you for coming, *Frau* Kaufmann," she said, her voice low, almost apologetic. "Under the circumstances, I don't want to keep you long. We invited you here to discuss your son. Albert is a bright little boy-"

Mrs. Kaufmann's eyes widened. "Is everything all right? Albert didn't get into trouble, did he?"

Mrs. Rosner's brows shot up, her surprise obvious. "Why, of course not. Albert is a sweet little boy. So quiet. A real angel."

"Oh." The young woman sank back into her chair with a relieved sigh.

Curious, Rafe tilted his head as he watched her, the way the emotions played across her expressive face. "Why would you ask if he'd gotten into trouble?"

She shook her head, looking confused. "I don't know. I just...I thought he was acting out at school like he was at home."

Rafe frowned. "Acting out?"

"Yes, throwing tantrums, ripping up his books, deliberately breaking his toys. Ever since David died…" her voice trailed off, her face taking on a forlorn look. "Albert can't understand why his papa went away and won't come back."

Slowly, Rafe nodded. He hadn't been wrong. The sadness he'd seen in the child had been due to the loss of his father. At Albert's age, no matter how his mother must have tried to explain, it would be hard for him to understand why he would never see his father again. That explained his displays of anger when he was at home where he felt safe enough to vent his true feelings. At school, though, his pain was manifested in his silence, his withdrawal from play, and his permanent look of sadness.

"That certainly explains things," Mrs. Rosner said. "We noticed how tense he was, and how very sad. We just didn't realize he'd recently gone through such loss. Thank you for sharing that with us, *Frau* Kaufman. I know it was difficult."

The woman nodded in acknowledgment, but she didn't say anything. Mrs. Rosner did not press. Then, as if prompted by a motherly instinct, the matron reached over and patted the younger woman's clasped hands.

Mrs. Kaufman did not say a word, but she nodded, her lips trembling like she was trying hard not to cry. After several seconds, she bit down on her lip, drew in a shuddering breath, then glanced up and gave Mrs. Rosner a look that told of the gratitude she felt for the other woman's show of sympathy.

Now, understanding the situation, they did not keep Mrs. Kaufman long. Within twenty minutes, they were wrapping up after having worked out a specific plan of support for the little boy. The teachers would make special effort to draw him out and get him involved in class activities. However, if he resisted, they would take it slow and give him space, understanding that it could take time.

An important component of the plan, though, was to have him spend some time with someone skilled in helping children work through the grief of the loss of a parent. Such therapy was critical at this stage. If Albert had a predisposition toward anxiety, early intervention should prove effective in preventing the later development of such issues as depression and mood or sleep disorders.

Until this professional help was scheduled Rafe had a plan of his own. He had been looking out for the little tyke in the short space of time he'd known him but now he would pay even closer attention. It wasn't that he had to. He wanted to. The sad little face pulled at his heart strings, and he would do anything in his power, limited though it might be, to soften the blow and make Albert smile again.

So, with that goal in mind, Rafe spent the rest of the week caring for his group, but keeping his eye out for any opportunity to get Albert more involved. By Friday, he'd found the perfect strategy.

Albert was most engaged when he'd been assigned an important task, something that gave him a sense of control. Now, in his new job as coloring monitor, he made sure that the little blue bin was always filled with crayons and the coloring books were distributed right on time. After Friday's coloring session, he quickly gathered up the books and materials and put them away. It seemed that the new responsibility kept him busy, and, more importantly, it took his mind off his personal problem.

After he'd shoved the supplies into the cupboard, Albert pushed the door shut, then turned to look at Rafe, his gaze hesitant.

Immediately, Rafe dropped to his knees where he could be closer to the little boy's level. He gave him a reassuring smile and held up his hand, palm outward. "Great job, my man," he said, with a satisfied nod. "Gimme five."

As if his teacher had just offered him the greatest treat in the world, Albert's face broke into a wide smile. Not waiting another second, he ran over and gave Rafe a hearty slap right in the middle of his palm.

And what Rafe saw made his heart melt. It took some effort not to pull the child into a big bear hug. For the first time since he'd met Albert, the child was giving him a smile that actually lit up his eyes.

And, if for nothing else, Rafe knew that his decision to come to the Coleman School had been the right one. He had no regrets.

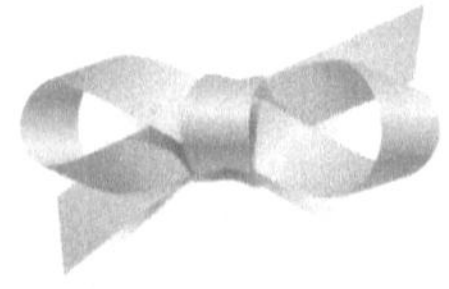

CHAPTER TEN

WHAT THE HECK WAS THE matter with Rafe Kent? Why was he ignoring her? Anya shook her head, totally annoyed. But it wasn't Rafe she was annoyed with. It was with herself.

Because he was doing exactly what she wanted, wasn't he? He was staying away from her, and that was exactly what any sane woman in her situation would want. Except that, apparently, she wasn't sane. Not anymore, anyway. She couldn't be, if the more aloof he became, the more she wanted him. But why should she want a man like Rafe, when she knew exactly what his type was like?

"How dumb can you get?" she muttered to herself, and then, ignoring her own reprimand, she walked across the room to where Claire Rosner sat at her desk in the staff room.

"So, Claire," she said, as she stood there clasping her hands in front of her, wondering how best to broach the subject, "uhm, how are things working out in your classroom? I haven't seen your assistant today. How's he managing with the babies?"

Claire looked up from her papers and her face broke into a warm smile. "Everything's going splendidly," she gushed. "I couldn't have asked for a better assistant."

Curious, Anya raised her brows. "What do you mean?"

"I tell you, Anya, Rafe is a dream with the children, and especially with a special one who's going through some personal challenges." Her face turned serious. "It's so sad but he recently lost his father. It's been tough on the little one, but Rafe has taken him under his wing. You should see the positive impact he's made on Albert in the short space of only two weeks."

"Really? What did he do?" For some reason, Anya couldn't picture Rafe as the type to relate to a grief-stricken child.

"He's been exceptional with the children," Claire said, "and especially with Albert. So tender and caring. The way he works with him, paying attention to him every step of the way, you would think the child was his own. One day, he's going to make a wonderful father. I have no doubt about that."

"Oh, really." Anya said the words slowly, in a soft, distracted whisper as her mind absorbed what Claire had just said. Rafe? The type to make a good father? Had Claire really seen that in him? She was finding that hard to believe. "And the little one who lost his father, is he all right now?"

Claire shook her head. "No, I wouldn't say that, but he's doing a lot better than he was when he just got here. Rafe is slowly drawing him out of his shell, getting him involved in class activities. He even came up with the idea of giving him responsibilities in the classroom and we've seen some good results from that. Now, he tells the other children he's Teacher Rafe's helper." She chuckled. "That's what Rafe calls him. His little helper elf."

Anya was nodding slowly again, the words sinking in. Claire was usually good at reading people, and she'd spent the past two weeks working with Rafe, so it made sense to pay attention to what she was saying about him. The only problem was, this picture was not gelling with the one she'd formed in her head. Which one was right? Or could he be both?

When Anya glanced back at Claire, there was a curious look in the older woman's eyes. "Are you all right, dear?" she asked. "You look like something's on your mind."

"No, nothing." Anya tried to look nonchalant. "So, where's Rafe?" she asked, her tone deliberately casual.

"Oh, he'll be back soon. By late afternoon," Claire said, as she sat back in her chair, folded her arms and looked up at Anya. "I sent him to that half-day retreat they're having for new recruits. He shows real promise as a teacher. I think the session will be good for him." She was speaking casually, but in her eyes was a knowing look that made Anya glance away. She had no intention of letting Clairvoyant Claire read her mind.

"Well, I'll catch you later," she said, making ready to escape. "I've got some things to finish up before I go."

When she was safely back at her own desk, Anya opened the drawer and pulled out her sticky notepad. On the top sheet, she wrote one simple sentence, 'Can we talk', signed her name and ripped the paper off the pad. Then, before she could chicken out she folded it and, coolly and casually, she walked to the other end of the staff room, acting like she'd gone over there to have a look out the window. Making sure no one was looking, especially Mrs. Know-It-all Claire, she slipped the paper onto Rafe's desk and shifted his paperweight on top of it. Then, cool as cucumber, she sauntered back to her desk, sat down, and pretended to be absorbed in the lesson plans she'd been working on.

Soon, though, she wasn't pretending. She became so caught up in what she was doing, that she didn't notice the passing of time, and it was only when she heard heavy, unmistakably male footsteps across the room that she looked up from her work. Immediately, her heart jerked.

It was Rafe, back from his off-campus meeting, looking so serious, so handsome and...so distant. He walked right by her desk, and even as she gazed up at him, all he spared her was a curt nod.

Anya dropped her gaze then bit her lip. Talk about embarrassing. Here she was, eager to see this man – stupidly eager, if she should admit it to herself – and he, on the other hand, hardly even noticed. He might have had an interest before, but he'd gotten over it pretty quickly. That much was obvious. Painfully so.

And now, as if that weren't bad enough, he would go to his desk and find her note. And how would he react to that? Would he crumple it and throw it in the bin or, even worse, would he laugh? Anya cringed at the thought. Feeling mortified, even though it hadn't happened yet, she began to pack up her papers, ready to stuff them into her shoulder bag. She would finish her work at home. She couldn't stay there a minute longer.

And before she left, she wouldn't even look over at him. If she saw him laughing at her, or saw even just a smirk on his face, she would never live it down. Before it came to that, she would just slip out and hope he would forget she'd ever written him that stupid note. Oh, why had she been so-

"Yes. How's this evening for you?"

Anya gasped, and her head jerked up. Rafe was standing there, right beside her desk and he was smiling down at her.

"Yes?" she whispered, not knowing what else to say.

"Yes," he said, again. "We can talk. I would love that. Can we go somewhere after work? What would be convenient for you?"

Quickly, Anya searched her mind. Somewhere nearby, somewhere quiet, but a public place. She still wasn't sure she could trust him. She had to check him out some more. "What about the Bremen Public Library? I need to go there to return some books. We could talk there."

He raised an eyebrow, looking amused. "The library? I haven't been inside one of those in a while, but why not?

"I can meet you at the reference desk at four o'clock. The library is open until six on Fridays. More than enough time for us to talk." As Anya spoke, she was pushing her chair back, wanting to get away. He was standing there, so close, making her so aware of him, she was finding it hard to think straight. Right the, she needed to put some distance between them. She needed to get away, to think, to prepare herself. Later, she would be ready.

Quickly, she grabbed her bag and stood up, but, finding herself even closer to him, she took a quick step back. She felt the color rise in her face. There was no way he hadn't noticed that move.

She forced a smile. "Okay, so I'll see you at four, then. Catch you later."

Then, before he could say a word, she turned and headed for the door. She did not pause until she was safely in the front seat of her car. There, she sagged against the steering wheel.

Goodness, she'd just done something so out of character for her. She'd just asked Rafe Kent out. Mind you, it was only to the public library, but still, a date by any other name was still a date.

She only hoped she hadn't started something she wouldn't know how to finish.

. . ❧ . .

ANYA WAS THE EASIEST person to find. It wasn't just that she was standing exactly where she'd said she would be, right in front of the library's main reference desk. The thing was, as soon as Rafe came within five yards of her, once he was in the same room, his skin would tingle. Literally.

It was the strangest thing, and if anybody had told him that could happen, he would have laughed them into the ground. He would never have believed it...until it happened to him.

Over the past week and a half, he'd had to be a darned good actor to hide from Anya how he really felt. Seeing her everyday, walking right by her in the staff room and the lounge, it hadn't been easy. He'd had to act cool, when all he'd wanted to do was take her some place where they could be alone, and then kiss her till she promised never to run away again.

But now, it looked like his efforts had paid off. He was going to be meeting with Anya, and she'd been the one to set up the rendezvous. When he'd seen her note, he'd had a hard time hiding his goofy grin. Anya was coming around at last.

She must have sensed his presence because, before he even got to her, she turned, and her eyes were not on the people passing by. No, she was looking directly at him, like she'd known the exact moment he entered the area. To his relief, when she saw him, her face brightened. "Hi," she said, as he walked up to her. "You're right on time. Thanks."

His lips curled in a smile, and he shrugged. "Of course. How could I keep a beautiful woman waiting?" He was amused when she looked away, a soft blush coloring her cheeks. She actually looked embarrassed. He had no doubt that many men before him had told her the same thing, but her modesty made his compliment special nonetheless. Or could it be something more? Dared he think that her reaction wasn't so much due to the words, but to the fact that they'd come from him?

Wanting to lighten the moment, he made a feeble attempt at a joke. "So, you want us to talk, and this is the place you choose? If we start talking, the librarians will be shooing us out of here before we can blink."

That made her smile. "No, they won't. I have the perfect place. It's my study spot in a far-off corner. No-one ever goes there."

"And what if today's different?" he asked, shaking his head at her confidence. "Someone could be in 'your spot' at this very moment."

"Nope. I made sure that wouldn't happen. I already marked it. My jacket, my book bag and my notebooks are spread out all over the table there."

"Ah-ha." Rafe nodded. "Well planned, I see."

She smiled. "You could say that."

Rafe followed Anya to the spot she'd designated as their meeting place. It was a cozy little area with a couple of comfortable-looking armchairs facing a low mahogany table on top of which Anya's things were scattered. He recognized the jacket she'd worn to school earlier that day.

Immediately, she went over to what must have been her favorite chair. She sank into it with such casual familiarity that he could just imagine the number of hours she'd spent in that seat, studying or working or just relaxing with a good book.

Anya waved her hand at him. "Have a seat."

He did as she ordered, and he took up residence in the armchair facing hers, then leaned back and propped his elbows on the arms. He watched her as she reached over and picked up her book bag then fidgeted with the clasp even as she avoided his eyes. He could see she was nervous. Conversation would probably put her at ease, but he'd never been one for small talk, and he wasn't about to start now. Tenting his fingers, he fixed his gaze on her. "So, what are we going to talk about?"

For just a second, she hesitated, but then, as if gathering her courage about her, she met his gaze head on. "You."

Surprised, Rafe raised his eyebrows. "Me?"

She nodded. "Ever since we met, I've been trying to figure you out. Tell me, who's the real Rafe Kent?"

"The real...?" Rafe couldn't help laughing. "I didn't know there was a fake one."

She tilted her head to one side as she regarded him, a serious expression on her face. "Sometimes I wonder. First, you carry yourself like some penniless wanderer, then you tell me you're a businessman, and now this. So what are you going to tell me this time? That you've always had a passion for teaching?"

He gave her a guilty grin. "I can't say it was a passion for teaching that brought me here. Passion, yes, but for something other than teaching." His voice turned soft. "Or maybe I should say someone."

The words made her color some more, but this time, she did not drop her gaze. "I know how you feel about me," she said, her voice tense. "What I don't get is how easily you switch from charming to belligerent, and now to caring and concerned."

"Excuse me?" Rafe frowned, one word in her speech jumping out at him, and it wasn't a pleasant word, by any means. "Belligerent? Why would you say that?"

"All right, maybe belligerent wasn't the right word, but you would have been...if I'd given you the chance." The look Anya gave him was full of challenge.

Confused, Rafe sat forward in the chair, his frown deepening. "I don't get it. When was I ever-"

"Oh, don't give me that." Anya threw him a disdainful look. "Don't act like you don't remember."

When all he did was stare back at her in confusion, she continued. "That time you showed up at the seniors' center. Because I didn't want to stay and talk, you actually lifted your hand to me. How could you?"

Now Rafe was past confused. "What the devil are you talking about? I would never lift my hand to a woman." He drew back, suddenly feeling sick to the stomach. "Do you really think I would ever hurt you? Is that what you think of me?"

At his words, a look of uncertainty flitted across her face. "But...but you did try. When you showed up, and I asked if you didn't take no for an answer, you got so angry. I could see it on your face. And then you came toward me, and you looked like you were going to raise your hand."

"Anya, Anya, please. Never say that again. Don't even think it." It was all Rafe could do not to reach out and take her hand. He wanted desperately to reassure her, to make her understand how wrongly she'd judged him, but he knew that trying to touch her would be a big mistake. His words would have to do. "I have never in my life put my hand on a woman in anger. That's not who I am. I was angry, yes, but not with you. I was angry with my friends for tricking me into going to the center to see you. And I was angry with myself, for falling for it like a fool. I should have known not to trust those idiots." He sighed. "Even if I moved toward you, it wasn't to hurt you. And I was only lifting my hands like this." He raised his hands, palm upward. "It was an innocent gesture. I just wanted to explain."

Anya was staring at him, the look of disbelief still lingering, her eyes narrowing, as if she were trying to figure him out. And then, to his relief, her face began to clear. "Oh," she said, and just like that, her tone nonchalant. "I guess I jumped to conclusions. Sorry."

"So...you believe me?" Now, it was Rafe's turn to stare, as he sat there, trying to figure her out.

Anya gave a little grimace, then she nodded. "I believe you. I guess I was too wound up when I thought you were defying what I'd told Khalil, about not having you track me down. I thought he'd told you, but you'd decided to come, anyway." Then, she sighed. "And I may have also used another man's fat to fry you."

"Come again?"

She shook her head. "It's a situation with my neighbor. I had to rescue her a few times from her abusive husband. I guess I was using his behavior to judge you. That wasn't fair. I'm sorry."

Slowly, he nodded. "I'm just glad that's cleared up. I want you to know that I would never do anything to hurt you."

She gave him a tiny smile. "That's a whole lot easier to believe after what I heard about you."

"You heard something about me?" Rafe tensed again. He could only hope that what she'd heard was the truth, and not some blown-out-of-proportion story like what Lion had fed her about the many women he had all over Europe.

She chuckled. "Don't worry. It's all good. Claire told me how good you are with Albert, how you're drawing him out of his shell."

"Oh, that." He suppressed a sigh of relief. "It's nothing."

"No," she said, shaking her head, "it's something. Something really important. You're making a difference in that little boy's life. And do you want to know something?" She gave him an enigmatic look.

"What?"

"The only reason I asked you out was because of what Claire told me. That was what made me realize I might have misjudged you. That's why I wanted to talk to you about that incident, to really understand what happened." She gave him a cautious smile. "I just knew that couldn't be the real you."

He smiled back. "I'm glad *Frau* Rosner isn't the type to keep things to herself. I owe her one."

Anya's smile deepened. "You owe her a lot. It's because of her that I decided you may take me out on a date tomorrow night."

Rafe cocked an eyebrow, his smile widening. "You decided?" Then, he laughed. "Is that your way of asking me out on a date?"

"Maybe. You could say, I'm the kind of woman who likes to take charge." She gave him a cheeky grin. "Even if it means roughing up a man sometimes."

Rafe shook his head. "I don't know if I like the sound of that. Is it really safe to be around a woman like you?"

"Let's put it this way," she said, her look direct and bold. "You'll probably be safer with me than with any other woman you've ever met. I don't have a blue belt in karate for nothing."

Raising his brows in mock fright, Rafe drew back in his chair. "Ooh, I'm really scared now."

Anya laughed. "Oh, shut up." She pulled her notepad out of her bag, ripped off a piece of paper, and handed it to him. "Now, write this down. This is where you will meet me tomorrow at seven. And make sure you're not late, or else." She gave him what she must have thought was a stern look, but to him, it looked so cute.

And, just like that, he had another date with Anya all lined up, not due to his pretense at ignoring her but because of something that, ironically, had been out of his control. Anya had come around because of his show of concern for a child, something he'd done without any intention of impressing her, or anyone. He'd simply done it because he cared.

In the end, though, he was glad how things had worked out. And if things continued to work in his favor, by tomorrow night, he would get the kiss he'd been craving far too long.

CHAPTER ELEVEN

WHEN SATURDAY EVENING came, Anya dressed carefully, wanting to look so different, she would take Rafe's breath away. As she sat in front of the mirror, she smiled at the thought. Maybe it was a bit presumptuous of her to think that way, but she wanted to at least surprise him. So far, all he'd seen her wearing were work clothes or sweat pants. Tonight, she would wear an emerald-green cocktail dress, one she was told made her hazel eyes sparkle. It was a man who'd told her that, so who knew if he'd been telling the truth or had just been trying to get on her good side? Still, true or false, she was going to take his word for it and hope Rafe would see whatever it was that man had seen.

She slid her feet into her four-inch-high soft suede pumps, grabbed the matching purse, and headed for the stairs. She'd warned Rafe not to be late. After all of that, she'd better make sure she wasn't, either.

When Anya got to Bremer Ratskeller, she had to smile. She'd deliberately headed out early enough so that she could arrive at least fifteen minutes before their meeting time, but when she walked in, it was to see Rafe already there. "You beat me to it," she said, as she walked over to him. "Very obedient, I see."

"Yes, ma'am," he said, with a bow. "I don't take chances with anyone who can kick my butt."

"Smart," she said, giving him a nod. "Very smart. Now, let's go see if our table is ready. We may as well get started early." Then, she chuckled. "And anyway, I'm starving."

Rafe stepped aside. "Lead the way."

After they'd been seated, Rafe looked around. "So, this is the old wine cellar." He nodded. "Impressive. It's got a certain ambiance I like."

Anya nodded. "Its own special charm. That's why I love it." Then, she leaned forward. "And guess what?" she said, in a conspiratorial whisper. "They've got a wine list that would keep you happy for a year."

Smiling, he shook his head. "I'm probably the only person it wouldn't keep happy. I don't drink."

Anya raised her eyebrows. That was a surprising tidbit. "A teetotaler? I wouldn't have thought it." Then, as her mind went back to their first date, she nodded slowly. "Come to think of it, last time we went out, all you had was water. Now I know why. Any special reason you don't drink?"

He shrugged. "I never had the inclination to. I tried beer once, hated it, and just decided to forget the whole bit." He shook his head. "And talking about reason, from what I saw in college, drinking and reason don't fit in the same sentence."

She grinned. "You're as strait-laced as they come. Boy, you're certainly full of surprises." Anya meant what she said. Rafe was gentle with children, it seemed like he respected women, and he didn't feel he had to drink to have a good time. Surprises like these, she could deal with. She certainly wasn't going to complain. As Claire had so rightly hinted, he was looking more and more like 'father material' every day.

That thought made her feel warm inside. Earlier, she'd thought she was being presumptuous when she wanted to impress him with her clothes, but if ever there were thoughts that were presumptuous, it had to be the ones she was thinking just then. Thank goodness Rafe couldn't read minds.

Right at that moment, the server approached their table, which was a good thing, because her thoughts were getting too risqué for her own comfort. Next thing you knew, she would be blushing, and then he would be asking her why. And how could she tell him the truth?

After she'd ordered, Anya decided to use the opportunity to learn even more about Rafe. She was coming to realize that the man was like a deep pool, and it was only by plumbing its depths that you'd find the real Rafe. She planned to do just that.

"How long have I known you, Rafe?" she asked the question out of the blue, making him glance up in surprise.

"We first met back in early May," he said, giving her a quizzical look, "so that makes it almost four months. Why?"

"I'm just thinking," she said, drawling the words, "that I've known you all this time, but I don't really know you. Know what I mean?"

He chuckled. "Not really, but I'm more than willing to tell you whatever you want to know." He sat back in his chair. "Shoot."

"Hmm. Where do I start?" She gave him a mischievous smile. He'd said he would answer whatever she asked. She would hold him to that. "Tell me," she said slyly, "about the broken hearts you left all over Europe." Then, she laughed. "Just kidding. I won't even go there. Tell me…," she said slowly, drawing out the words again to tease him, "…about you. About your family. I want to know what's made you, you."

"No problem." Rafe looked unperturbed by any of her questions. "I grew up on a farm in Iowa, the youngest of four brothers, all of us adopted by Maggie and Bill Kent. Ransom's the oldest, then there's Ridge, then Ryder, then me."

"All boys. I'm going to guess you and your brothers were a rambunctious bunch."

"Tell me about it. Sometimes we would drive Mom crazy. Actually, it was mostly the others. I was the angel of the family."

"Were you really an angel?" Anya shook her head. "The way you say it, I wonder…"

Rafe laughed. "No, I was actually the black sheep of the family. Still am."

"You? Are we talking about the same man who spent extra time with a little boy, trying to help him deal with his grief? Are we talking about the same man who thinks nothing of wiping snotty little noses, soothing bumps and bruises and drying tears? Somehow, I don't see 'black sheep' there."

"Thanks for your vote of confidence. Come tell all of that to my family, will you? I'm not sure they'd believe you, though." He gave her a rueful grin. "They kinda think I'm the brat in the family, and I can't tell a lie. I've given them plenty of reason."

"Well, whatever you did to make them think that way, you've changed." Anya was adamant. "You're kind and caring and mature, and the children could not want a better teacher."

Rafe gave her a look of surprise. "Wow. I really need to take you back to Iowa. With you singing my praises, I'll be son number one, for sure."

At his words, Anya realized how star-struck she must have sounded, and she blushed. Where had all that come from? She hadn't meant to gush like that.

"Maybe," he said, cutting into her thoughts, "it's because I've been associating with the right kind of people. People like you."

What was he trying to do? Turn her pink as a petunia? Needing some kind of distraction, she reached for the wine list, and then she remembered he didn't drink. Under those circumstances the list wouldn't be much of a discussion topic, would it?

But then, he rescued her with a question. "Since I got back to Bremen, this is the first time I'm getting the chance to ask about your summer vacation. How was it? Did anything special?"

Relieved that he'd changed the subject, Anya shrugged. "Nothing out of the ordinary. I spent a week with my father in Bonn and a week with mom. She's in New York. What with Helga calling me every day to cry over her crazy husband, the time away did me some good."

"Who's Helga? And what's that about a crazy husband?"

"Helga's my neighbor. She lives across the street. Her husband..." Anya paused, not wanting to be discussing her neighbor's private life, but then she relaxed. It wasn't like Rafe knew her, anyway. "Her husband is abusive, so I encouraged her to make a police report. She got a restraining order, so he had to leave the house, but then she called me every day for three weeks straight, crying that she missed him."

"A man who was abusing her?"

"You would think she would be glad to see the back of him, right?" Anya shook her head. "Anyway, it got to the point where I had to get away. It was just too much." Then, she gave a tiny grunt. "And if that weren't bad enough, I ended up having to take out a restraining order against her husband, too."

That caught Rafe's attention. He sat forward in his chair, a frown darkening his face. "Explain that one," he said, his voice brusque. "Was that man harassing you, too?"

Anya grimaced. "You could say that. Just the other day, he woke me up after three in the morning, pounding on my door, cursing me out. He blames me for his wife finally throwing him out."

"What?"

"Yeah, he does. That night, he made such a racket, that I wasn't the only one who ended up calling the police. Lots of neighbors heard him, too. When the police picked him up off my back porch, he was stinking drunk."

"Jeez. Suppose he'd broken in?"

"He wasn't armed. I could see that. If he'd put one foot in my house, I would have defended myself. That's all I'm going to say."

"Tough words, Anya, but you're a woman living alone. I don't like-"

"Don't worry about it, Rafe. I'm not stupid. That's why I took out the restraining order. And if he ever shows up again," she said, eyes narrowing, "I'll be ready for him."

Rafe was shaking his head, and to her chagrin, he wasn't looking impressed by her bravado. "Listen, I don't want you to take this lightly. Do you have an alarm system installed?"

"No, I never thought of having one."

"Get one installed immediately." Rafe's tone brooked no argument. "I don't want you to take any chances with this guy."

"Okay, okay, I won't." Anya was almost beginning to regret she'd even mentioned the incident. All of a sudden, Rafe was Mr. Super Protective, and independent spirit that she was, it was beginning to grate on her nerves.

"I know what you're thinking," Rafe said, startling her. "I can see it in the way you set your lips just now. You're a stubborn little cuss, but I'm not going to stop bugging you until you get it done. I'll come over and install it myself, if I have to."

"A stubborn little what? What did you just call me?" Anya was trying hard to look offended, but she couldn't help the grin that was slipping in to spoil it. "Is that some kind of American insult?"

"Don't you worry about that." He was the one giving the stern look. "I'm not going to let you leave this restaurant until you promise me you'll do as I say."

"What? You're going to tie me to the chair?" she challenged, giving him a look of defiance.

"I'll do better than that," he whispered, his voice now low and silky soft. "I'll..."

He broke off and the seductive look he'd been giving her suddenly disappeared. It was when he glanced up and nodded that she knew why. The server was heading their way. It was dinnertime.

After that, Rafe didn't bring up the alarm system argument again. Anya almost wished he would. The way his golden eyes flashed when he'd met her challenge, the way his voice turned smooth and sexy, the promise he'd been about to make...they'd been such a turn-on. Rafe could not have known it, but at that moment if he'd said he would kiss her...or more...she wouldn't have said no.

Later that evening, when they couldn't stretch out the dinner then dessert then tea and coffee then dinner mints any longer, Rafe reached across the table and touched her hand. "It's after eleven o'clock," he said. "I think I've kept you out long enough. Little girls need their sleep."

Anya sighed. She wished she could object, but he was right. It wouldn't be wise to be going home alone after midnight. She nodded, sorry that their evening had come to an end. She could only hope there would be more of the same. And hopefully, next time he would be the one doing the asking.

Although she'd said it was her treat, Rafe called for the bill and as they walked out of the restaurant and toward the parking lot, he rested his hand lightly under her elbow, sending tingles up her body. It felt so good, and yet so disconcerting. Was he feeling it, too?

They got to her car and Anya turned to say goodbye. "Thank you," she said softly. "I had a wonderful evening."

"Not so fast, little one."

Rafe surprised her when he placed a finger under her chin and tilted her face up toward his. Was he going to kiss her?

"Do you think I'm letting you go like that? Wait here," he said. "I'll get my car. I'm going to follow you home and make sure you get in safe."

When Anya realized she wasn't going to get the kiss she was craving, her heart sank. Just a little. She could only take consolation in knowing they weren't saying goodbye. Not just yet.

As he'd promised, Rafe drove behind her, following the whole eight miles back to her home. When she parked on the street in front of the house, he pulled in right behind her, and when she got out of her car, he did the same, then he took her hand and walked her right to her door.

But when Rafe turned her to face him, and he put that same long, lean finger under her chin, this time, she knew exactly what he wanted. Wanting the kiss, maybe even more than he did, she closed her eyes and waited for his lips to touch hers. When they did, she groaned. They felt so good.

Rafe's lips were warm and mobile, firm but gentle, insistent then teasing. As he kissed her, he slid his arms around her waist, pulling her close, so close she could feel the heat radiating from his body.

Her nipples pebbling in response, Anya did as he had done, sliding her arms around him, moving even closer until their bodies touched, and then she was pressing against him, giving herself over to the kiss, feeling every ripple of his muscled torso stamped into her chest.

When Rafe finally relaxed his hold, releasing her from his embrace, he was breathing hard. He closed his eyes for a second, and it looked like he was trying to regain his composure. "I'd better let you go, little one," he said, his voice husky, "or else I won't be able to stop."

Anya nodded and let out a soft sigh. "And there I was," she said, with a smile, "planning to invite you in for a cup of coffee." At his look of disbelief, she shook her head, and laughed. "Just kidding."

He chuckled. "You'd better be. You wouldn't be that reckless. Now, go inside. I want to see you safely in, with the door locked."

Anya sighed again. She really did want to invite him in, but she knew when to stop. It would be stupid to tempt fate.

"All right, boss. Whatever you say." On an impulse, she stood on tiptoe and gave him a quick peck on the cheek. "Goodnight," she whispered, then turned, unlocked the door, and slipped inside.

Rafe did not walk away until Anya had locked the door behind her, and he did not drive away until she was upstairs and had turned on the light in her bedroom. Only then, did she hear the engine turn over and the car drive away.

And as Anya sat on her bed to take off her shoes, she was smiling. She'd been defensive and a little bit annoyed when he'd acted protective, but now she was loving it. He'd come all this way just to make sure she was safe.

She'd been thinking of him as father material, but now, it seemed he was a whole lot more. Rafe was definitely husband material, too. She would bet her money on that.

CHAPTER TWELVE

THE TENSION WAS ALMOST too much. After their date Saturday night, Rafe waited anxiously for Sunday to pass so he could see Anya again. Big mistake. Instead of cooling his desire to be with her, seeing her at the school only heightened it. It was hell, seeing her in the staff room and the teachers' lounge, and only being able to give her a simple greeting and make small talk. Every time he saw her, he wanted to pull her into his arms and kiss her again. With nowhere on the compound where they could even find the privacy to have quiet conversation, all they could do was smile, nod and exchange a word or two.

Rafe knew he could have asked to see Anya somewhere off campus during the week, but he wouldn't go there. She was a busy woman, a teacher with tons of responsibilities. It would be unfair to ask her out in the middle of the week. This weekend, though, he was determined to spend time with her.

And so, when Friday came around, he made sure to make her understand that she was already booked for Saturday at five so she shouldn't make any plans.

"Is that an order, *Herr* Kent?" she asked cheekily.

"It's an order, *Fraulein*. And this time, we're not driving separate cars. I'm picking you up. Be ready by five. Or else."

That made her raise her eyebrows. "Ooh," she whispered. "Laying down the law, are we? Don't you worry. I'll be ready."

"Oh, and dress casual. We're going to a movie."

"No problem."

On Saturday, Rafe was at Anya's door, banging the knocker, at exactly five o'clock. Within seconds, she was opening up like she'd been hanging around nearby, just waiting for him to arrive. Wishful thinking, probably, but it felt good to even think that she was as anxious to see him as he was to see her.

"You're ready, I see. Good. I came prepared to mete out punishment if you were late."

She gave him a crooked grin. "And what kind of punishment were you planning to mete out?"

"Don't ask," he said, deciding to be coy. If he ever told her what he had in mind, she would probably seek refuge inside her house and never come out. Better to keep that one to himself.

To his surprise, Anya didn't look like she was going to bother taking a handbag or purse for the evening's rendezvous. "I've got everything I need right here," she said. She dug into the back pocket of her jeans and pulled out her cell phone. From the other pocket, she pulled out a few euros, then she patted the breast pocket of her jeans jacket. "Cell phone, keys and money for a taxi, just in case you get fresh, and I have to dump you on our date."

"Good thinking," he said, not the least bit perturbed by her contingency plan. "The way I'm feeling tonight, you might very well need that taxi money." He threw her a crooked grin. "But it will be all your fault for looking so delicious."

"In these old jeans?" The twinkle in her eyes told him she was enjoying their joshing.

"Especially in those jeans," was his answer. There was hardly anything sexier than a woman in a pair of form-fitting jeans.

As the sun dimmed with the coming evening, they hopped into his BMW and drove off to Weserpark. "I chose this mall because there's a movie that's showing that I think you'll like." Rafe steered the car into a parking spot.

"Oh? What is it?"

"It's an old movie, but it made me think of you. I was surprised it's still showing anywhere, but one of the movie theatres is having an old school weekend."

"So, what is it? Tell me already." Apparently, Anya didn't like being kept in suspense. She was looking like she wanted to pinch him to hurry him up.

"Okay, just hang on. Before I tell you what the movie is, I just want you to know it's not my usual thing. It's a girly movie but I think you'll like it."

Now, she was looking like she wanted to punch him, so he knew he'd better talk fast. "Okay, it's called 'The Bodyguard', a nineties movie starring Whitney Houston and Kevin Costner."

"So, you've cast yourself in the role of my bodyguard?" she asked, her tone teasing.

"Just the opposite," he said. "I was casting you in the role of my bodyguard. You're the only person I know who's a karate expert."

"Oh, you." This time, she really did punch him, but she didn't do too much damage. Just a tap on the biceps. Maybe she was just going easy on him.

The movie lasted longer than he'd thought, over two hours when he'd been expecting an hour and a half. But, just like he'd remembered from the time he'd first seen it, it was pretty entertaining. He'd just forgotten it was such a long chick flick. Still, if it got Anya into a mellow mood, it would be well worth it.

After the movie, from the way Anya leaned against him as they walked out of the theatre, he would say his strategy was a success. She was warming up to him, but even more important than that, she was beginning to trust him. When they walked through the mall together, she didn't wait for him to hold her hand. Instead, she took his, and when she looked up at him, there was no hesitation in her eyes. All her shyness was gone.

In the mall, they decided to forgo formalities and grab some chicken wings in sweet chili sauce from Thai Express.

"Let's take it to go," Anya suggested. "We can camp out on the rug in my living room and get our fingers all messy and sticky and not even worry about it."

"Whatever the lady desires." Rafe didn't need too much convincing. There was nothing he would like more than spending time on Anya's living room floor...although there were a lot more exciting things he could think of doing on that floor besides eating chicken wings. He smiled to himself at the thought, but he was also smiling because now he had no doubt that Anya saw him as a friend. Why else would she invite him into her home? Soon, though, he hoped they would be more than just friends...

Anya wasn't lying when she'd told him they'd be having dinner on the floor. At the door, they got rid of their shoes and donned fluffy indoor slippers, then padded off to the living room, where she spread a tablecloth. They sat on the floor across from each other, he with his legs stretching off to one side of the cloth, and she with her legs crossed lotus style. "Dig in," she ordered, and before he could make a move, she grabbed a chicken wing and took a hearty bite. He'd seen Anya eat before, and for a girl her size, she could really pack the food away. He wondered where she put it.

"What are you waiting for?" She licked a drop of sauce from her index finger. "Dibs on the fat one over there." She was reaching for her second chicken wing, and he hadn't even started yet.

"Hey, wait for me." Rafe could see that, if he didn't make a move, he was in danger of not getting any dinner at all.

She only laughed and grabbed the wing before he could get it.

After that, it was every man for himself, and of course, Anya got most of the goodies. Rafe wanted to think it was because he let her, but who was he kidding? The girl was quick, and she didn't play.

But then, after they'd had their fill, she was nice to him and served him a huge bowl of peach-flavored sherbet while she had the rainbow-colored one.

And then, as they sat there on the floor, watching each other lick the sweet stuff from their spoons, it came so naturally that they should lay their spoons down, both at the same time, and tilt forward, leaning toward each other, moving closer and closer until their lips touched.

Anya's lips were cool from the icy dessert she'd just eaten, but they were soft, so soft and yielding against his. Wanting to taste even more of her, Rafe leaned in further, until the gentle pressure of his lips nudged hers apart, and then he was truly tasting her, dipping into the heavenly nectar she'd been denying him all night. It was a heady sensation, and before he knew it, he was sliding his palms up her arms to cup the back of her head and tilt her body even more till she was off balance and clinging to him.

Rafe took full advantage of her helpless position. Sliding his other arm around her back, he drew her close, pulling her off her knees, sliding her across the rug and over onto his lap.

When he had her exactly where he wanted her, he stepped up his attack, kissing her with such passion that she clung desperately, and this time it wasn't because she was off balance. He could feel the frantic beat of her heart against his chest, and he knew the fire raging within him was consuming her, too.

When he withdrew his lips, she moaned, and it was all he needed to hear. She wanted more. Gathering her into his arms, he shifted his legs and got up, then strode over to the long, low couch pushed back against the wall. There, he laid her down, and as she sank into its plush depths, he sat down beside her, leaning over, but this time it wasn't to kiss her. This time, he wanted to feel her skin against his lips. He wanted to taste her. He wanted to know every inch of her.

As he trailed his lips down the side of her neck, Anya gave a soft sig and when he moved even further down to nibble at her collarbone, her sigh morphed into a moan. He slid lower still until his lips tickled the tops of her breasts, and that was when her soft moan deepened into a tortured groan.

Not wanting to move too fast,, he shifted his lips, moving back up toward her collarbone but her words stopped him.

"Please, Rafe," she whispered. "Don't stop. That feels so good."

Taking her plea as license to explore, he trailed a path back down to her breasts, feathering kisses along her heated skin, making her breath quicken and her fingers dig into his arms. When he slid his fingers up between them and he began to loosen the buttons on her shirt, she did not object. ,Instead, she arched her back and moaned again.

Soon Rafe had Anya's blouse open wide enough where he'd exposed her lace-covered breasts to his hungry gaze. In her jeans, he'd thought she was delicious,s but now she was mouth-watering. And he meant that in the literal sense of the word.

Ravenous now, he hooked his finger at the top of the right cup and drew it down until her precious pink bud popped into view. He lowered his head again, but slowly, ever so slowly, tormenting her until she arched her back again and reached her hands up to press his head down toward her. It was only then that he eased her misery, lowering his lips to her prettily puckered pebble, drawing it smoothly into his mouth, making her writhe in pleasure.

"Aah."

The relief sounding so sweet in that soft sigh, Rafe wanted to please her even more. He suckled at her nipple, then nibbled until she was gasping, then panting, in the pleasure from his lips.

"God, you're driving me crazy."

If only Anya knew that the words she'd whispered so fiercely described his own feelings exactly. Having her in his arms, his lips on her, his tongue tasting the sweetness of her skin, he knew he was in trouble. The hardness between his legs was painful testament to the torture he was enduring, wanting her so badly but knowing he must hold back. He wanted desperately to devour her,,,, but not yet, not now. This was Anya, his sweet, trusting Anya, and he knew if he moved too fast it could spoil everything. He couldn't take that chance.

Reluctantly, Rafe released Anya and drew back and when he gathered the fabric of her shirt in his hands this time it was to cover her and hide her from his gaze.

As he buttoned her shirt Anya stared up at him, her eyes cloudy with confusion. "Why did you stop?"

Rafe smiled and shook his head. "It's late," he said gently. "Time for little girls to get to bed."

He saw the look of disappointment in her eyes, but he didn't let it sway him. No matter how much he wanted her, he was a grown man, and he knew when it was time to exercise self-control...no matter that it hurt in more ways than one.

And, just so she would understand, he leaned over and gave her a soft kiss on the forehead. "You've had enough for one night, little one. Now, go get some rest." Then, before she could object, Rafe got up, gave her a little wave of farewell, then saw himself out.

Later, as he drove back to his apartment, the car eating up the Autobahn, Rafe could not help but think of how Anya had gotten off easy this time. With the way he felt about her, he knew that next time they found themselves together in an intimate setting like that, she would not be so lucky.

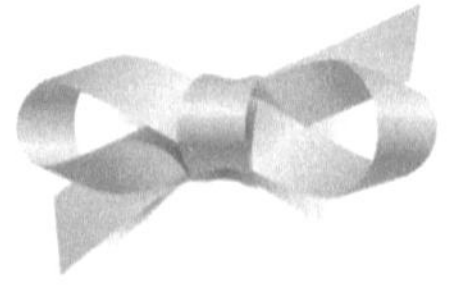

CHAPTER THIRTEEN

RAFE FELT LIKE GROANING out loud. He was sitting at the desk in the staff room, so that was not an option.

When they'd gone out on the weekend, why hadn't Anya mentioned that she would be away at a four-day teacher conference? He'd arrived at the school Monday morning, eager as a puppy. He couldn't wait to see Anya again. Instead, all he'd seen was her empty desk. When he'd enquired after her, it was only to be told that she wouldn't be in until Friday. Four whole days of waiting, and by day three, it was driving him crazy.

He had to stop thinking about Anya. Sure, he liked her...a lot...but this was past normal. This was an obsession. Clenching his teeth, he dug down into the work on his desk, trying desperately to lose himself in the preparation of his lesson plans; not that it was working. He almost wished something would go wrong with his business back in the States, so he would have reason to call and chew someone out. He needed distraction, anything to take his mind off missing Anya. But no, he would get no help from that end. Just when he wouldn't have minded a problem, everything with his business was going A-okay.

Thirty minutes later, his class full of children long gone, Rafe was still at his desk, but he'd gotten through most of his work,, and was now just working on the supplemental information for his lesson plan. He was surprised when he heard someone call his name and looked up to see the principal approaching, a woman with a familiar face close behind her. It was Mrs. Kaufman, Albert's mother.

Immediately, Rafe stood up to greet the ladies.

"Keep your seat," Mrs. Coleman said, waving him back down. "I just finished meeting with Mrs. Kaufman, and the way she sang your praises I just had to bring her over so she could tell you herself.

Rafe shook his head. "Please, there's no need-"

"No," the woman said, raising her hand to silence him. "I want to speak." A myriad of emotions flitted across her face, and she bit her lip and shook her head. When she finally spoke, her voice was raspy like she was close to tears. "I feel like I have a new child," she said. "I don't know what you've done to my son, but he's so different. It's like I have my old Albert back. Thank you. Thank you so much." This time, she lost her grip on the emotions she was trying to keep under control. Rafe heard her hiccup and then her hand flew to her mouth, and she bit down hard on her knuckles. Still, a sob escaped her throat, and a lone tear made its way down her cheek.

And if there was one thing Rafe couldn't stand, it was to see a woman cry. "Please," he said, and despite his boss's order, he got up from his chair. "Don't do that. I only did what any other teacher would have done."

"No," she said, giving her head an emphatic shake. "You did more than that. You showed interest in my son, and it unlocked his heart. Now, he's not scared to love again." She folded her hands in front of her. "There's a difference between duty and genuine interest, Mr. Kent, and children can tell the difference."

Mrs. Coleman smiled. "I don't see you finding an answer to that one, Rafe. Just accept the praise and say thank you."

"Uh, well, thank you, Mrs. Kaufman. And you're very welcome." And if that wasn't the height of embarrassment, Rafe didn't know what was. He sank back down into his chair, hating the fact that he was the center of attention. And what was worse, it was for doing something good. Notoriety he could take, but praise and tears were elements he could do without.

After the ladies had departed,- it took a while for Rafe to get back into work mode. In fact, it was damn near frustrating to get his mind back on lesson plans. It took him another ten minutes to concede defeat. Better to just pack up and head for home where he could think on Anya in peace.

Maybe it was a good thing he left when he did, because it was while at his apartment, that an idea came to him. Since a simple show of kindness had made such an impact on Albert, what if he were to organize a mentorship program for children who had lost a parent – or God forbid, both parents – in military combat?

The more he thought about it, the more the idea appealed to Rafe, and he knew that by the time he returned to the United States, it would be a done deal. He'd never liked the idea of going into business just for the sake of making money and this would be a worthwhile cause to support. He could hardly way to get it set up.

But then the thought of returning to the United States made him pause. What would that mean for his newfound relationship with Anya? And what was the nature of that relationship, anyway? He would almost say Anya felt for him the same way he felt about her. Still, one should never assume. When he saw her again, they would need to have a serious talk.

Maybe it wasn't a surprise that when Rafe finally saw Anya back at school on Friday, the plan to sit and have a serious talk was definitely not 'top-of-mind'. In fact, he totally forgot to lay that on the table. As soon as he spied her in the hallway, his heart jerked in his chest and he strode after her, his long legs letting him catch up with her in seconds. "Welcome back, Miss Petersen," he said, and when she turned and saw him, she was all smiles.

"Rafe. I went to the lounge looking for you."

"I was setting up the classroom," he said, his tone just shy of brusque. He couldn't help wondering how she could greet him with such a cheery face when she hadn't even bothered to tell him she was leaving.

"I thought as much. Hey, I'm running off to class right now, but can we talk after the children have left for the day? I'll see you later, okay?" And just like that, totally unapologetic, she turned and left him standing there in the middle of the hallway.

Rafe shoved his hands inside his pockets as he stared after her. That didn't go quite the way he was expecting. He would have thought she would open the conversation with an apology, even a quick one, followed by an explanation of her reason for keeping her seminar a secret. But no. Instead, she'd pushed him away until the afternoon. Okay...

Rafe kept himself busy all day, not wanting to dwell on Anya's return to school. As he kept telling himself, he was no kid. He needed to stop obsessing over this girl. Much good that self-talk did him. He was dying for the day to end so they could have that talk she'd promised.

And it was the torture of waiting for the hours to pass that made Rafe realize one thing – if ever he'd thought he was the one in control of this relationship, he was dead wrong.

. . ⁂ . .

ANYA WAS ONE HUNDRED percent satisfied with herself and she had good reason. She hadn't told Rafe she was going to be away most of the week, and it had been deliberate. If you wanted to get a man really interested in you, you couldn't be too easily accessible – not all the time. Sometime,s it was good to make a man miss you. Better yet, sometimes it was good to keep him wondering.

And that advice, compliments of her late *Oma*, was age-old and still relevant today. She'd proved that her grandmother's saying was true. If the look on Rafe's face was anything to go by, he'd been eaten up with musings about her all week. And he wasn't happy. She, on the other hand, could not have been more pleased.

That afternoon, Rafe lingered in the staff room as she finished up the tasks that had piled up on her desk. It was telling that even though it took her over an hour after the regular work time, he did not leave. When she finally packed up and gave him a wink, he quickly packed up his desk, too, and then he took her armful of books and papers and walked her to her car.

He didn't even wait for her to open the door or take her stuff from his arms. "So, what about that talk you said we should have? Do you want to talk now, or maybe we could go somewhere with more privacy?"

"Uhm." She stretched it out like she was in deep thought. "Why don't we wait until tomorrow to talk? There's no rush."

"No...what are you up to, Anya?" Eyes narrowed, his golden gaze was sharp as he stared down at her. "Is this some sort of game?"

"No, not at all. In fact..." she clicked the car door to unlock it, opened the back door, then reached for the pile of papers in Rafe's arms, "...this is very, very serious." She made sure to insert a hint of mystery into her voice. "And that's why I've decided this should wait until tomorrow." She gathered the papers into her arms then turned and dumped them on the back seat. When she turned back to him, she had a sly smile on her lips. "Pick me up tomorrow at eight. We're going dancing."

And then, not giving him the chance to respond, she stepped past him and hopped into the front seat of her car. "See you tomorrow," she said, with a wave, and then she was off, leaving Rafe standing, staring after her, his face the picture of consternation.

CHAPTER FOURTEEN

NUR FUR FREUNDE was rocking Saturday night. As one of Bremen's top electro clubs, it was the first place Anya thought of taking Rafe for a night of dancing and fun. She'd heard through the grapevine that *Moonbootica* would be spinning at the turntables, and she could think of no better way to spend the night than dancing to their DJ selections, with Rafe rocking along with her. If Anya had a vice, it had to be dancing and the fact that tonight she had the perfect person to go dancing with, made it even better.

Although, she had to admit, that perfect person looked sort of out of his depth. "Do you come here often?" he yelled, over the house music blasting in the club.

"Not so much, but when I can," she yelled back." "I love dancing."

His eyes were unreadable. "You hang here with your friends?"

She nodded. "When I was in university I used to come here a lot. Now that I'm working, I only come once in a while. And anyway, most of my friends moved away."

He gave her a look that told her she'd sparked his curiosity. "So, you come here...with other friends?"

She laughed. "No, I come alone. Just to dance."

Rafe was frowning now, and she could tell he didn't believe a word of it. "You come here alone?"

"Yes. Why?"

"And all these men hanging around here, they don't bother you?"

She waved her hand in dismissal. "Oh, them? I can handle them."

Now, his look of disbelief turned to one of incredulity. "You can handle them? I'd love to see that."

She chuckled. "They know me at this club, Rafe. They know better than to come mess with me. Want to know what they call me here?"

"What? Karate Kitten?" He laughed, looking pleased at his joke which was actually quite lame. She wouldn't tell him that, though.

"Nope. They call me Iron Fist. Want to know why?"

"Do I dare ask?" He gave her a look of mock fear.

She shrugged. "Okay, don't. I'll just show you. If a man invades my space, I ask him to let me hold his hand. Give me yours."

Without hesitation, he did. It was too easy. Rafe had walked into this one ,and he had no idea what he'd gotten himself into. She almost felt sorry for him.

As soon as their hands touched, Anya wrapped her fingers around his and then she squeezed and squeezed. And squeezed some more.

Like she knew it would, Rafe's face went from tan to red in seconds, and he tried to pull his fingers away, but it was no use. With the specialized muscle training she'd done in order to achieve a super strong grip, there was no way Rafe could escape. Not until she let him.

And then, because this was a man she actually liked, she did.

Rafe let out his breath in a whoosh. Then, he sucked in air and let it out again, like all the time she'd held him, she'd cut off his oxygen. "What the hell did you do that for?" he half yelled, half gasped. "Are you trying to kill me?"

Smiling, she shook her head. "Well, you didn't believe me, so I had to show you. Now, you know why the men – the sensible ones, anyway – stay away from me."

He nodded, giving her a pained look. "Now, I know."

Her smile deepened. "Now, you know."

After that, maybe it was because she felt a little bit guilty about playing that dirty trick on him, she was extra nice to Rafe, showing him all the latest dance moves and not laughing when he stumbled, and not saying a word even though it was painfully obvious that he would never make it to 'Dancing with the Stars'. Rafe was just too stiff to ever be a good or even passable dancer, but she didn't let that worry her. They were on the dance floor having fun, and that was all that mattered.

That night, Anya and Rafe didn't leave *Nur Fur Freunde* until way past midnight, and by that time, they were all discoed out.

As they walked back to his car, Rafe surprised her with his next comment. "I haven't had this much fun in a long time. Thank you."

That made her raise her eyebrows. "You're sure you had fun? You're not just saying that?" Then, when he nodded, she said, "And am I forgiven for abusing you?"

Rafe grimaced, as if the memory was still painful; then, he shook his head. "That, my dear lady, will not go unpunished."

Anya frowned, even though she wasn't the least bit perturbed by his threat. "What's that supposed to mean?"

"That's for me to know," he said softly, "and for you to find out."

"Hmm," was all she said in response. She was pretty confident that she could handle whatever he planned to dish out. She wasn't an expert in Rafe-ology for nothing. And by now, she could read him like a comic book. He wasn't that hard to figure out. So, that established, it was a confident Anya who hopped into the car beside him, and when they got to her house, as late as it was, she still had no qualms about inviting him in.

"Are you sure?" he asked, glancing at the clock on the dashboard. "Don't you think you'd better head to bed after all that dancing? You must be tired."

She rolled her eyes. "Please. You're talking to a girl who's used to partying till four in the morning. Now, come on." She jerked her head toward the house. "Let's have a nightcap."

Rafe looked doubtful, and Anya had to admit, she respected him for that. Most men would have jumped at the chance to enter her home in the middle of the night. After all, what better setting in which to seduce a maiden? She chuckled at the thought. Any man who wanted to seduce her had better have his A-game on. Anya Petersen could only be seduced if she wanted to be seduced, and the man trying would soon find that out. It took a minute, but the doubt on Rafe's face eventually dissipated and he shrugged. "Well, okay," he said. "If you insist." And then, he got out and came around to open her door.

Inside the house, Anya didn't have to give Rafe directions. He headed for the living room while she went off to the kitchen to get them some drinks, wine cooler for her and sparkling water for him. When she got back, he'd made himself comfortable on the floor, his back against the sofa, his long legs stretched out in front of him.

"What are you doing down there?" She placed the drinks on the table, straightened up, and dropped her hands casually on her hips. "Or didn't you notice the sofa behind you?"

"Don't be fresh, little girl," he gave her a crooked smile, "or else I'll have to spank you."

She didn't answer immediately. Instead, she cocked her head to one side and regarded him. He really was cute, especially now, with the collar of his shirt slightly askew from all that dancing, his hair which was beginning to grow long, again now curling at the collar of said shirt. A spanking from a guy who looked this good? She could live with that.

But that would have to wait just a minute longer. First, there was that little thing about quenching their thirst after a long night of dancing. She knelt down on the floor, right between his legs, and reached for the bottles on the coffee table.

By this time, Rafe's brows were raised in surprise. That was a good sign. She loved the idea of throwing him off balance. If she had any luck, she would keep him like that all night.

She put the first bottle to her lips and took long, slow sips of the fruit-flavored wine, her eyes never leaving his. Then, her thirst quenched, she laid the bottle back on the table. Now, it was his turn. She put the dewy bottle of sparkling water to Rafe's lips.

"Drink," she ordered.

Like a good little boy, he put his lips to the mouth of the bottle and sucked on the clear, cold water till he'd downed more than half. He must have been really thirsty. Now, it was time to see if he was just as thirsty for her.

Anya drew the bottle from Rafe's mouth,, and as he licked his lips, she reached out and placed his bottle on the table beside hers, all the while still holding his hooded gaze. Then, as seductively as she knew how, she closed her eyes, gave her lips a tiny pout and leaned forward, achingly slowly, until her lips touched his.

Rafe's lips softened at her touch, but outside of that, he didn't move. It was as if he wanted her to take control, and she did not mind that one bit.

Encouraged by his acquiescence, Anya leaned into him, letting her hands slide inside the collar of his shirt to clasp the warmth of his shoulders, pressing her lips against his until he moaned and gave her entrance. Then,,, as she tasted his tongue and the inner softness of his mouth she slid a hand up to clasp his nape, holding him immobile as she plundered his depths.

He moaned again and this time she released him, sliding her lips away until she was caressing the strength of his throat with the soft silkiness of her tongue. As she slid across to taste the sweet skin of his neck, his pulse beat an erratic rhythm beneath her lips.

Holding nothing back, Anya moved lower, intent on giving him all the pleasure he'd given her. There was no place for shyness now. Not tonight.

Quickly, she loosened the buttons on his shirt. Just like he'd done, she teased his chest with feathery kisses, then followed with a lascivious lick at a turgid nipple, and even as a groan escaped his lips, she was covering that stiff bud with her mouth, licking and sucking till he gasped and slid down on the ground, flat on the floor, and pulled her down on top of him.

"I want you," she whispered fiercely, and, showing no hesitation, she pushed the shirt off his shoulders, leaving his upper body bare to her gaze. What she saw made her lick her lips in anticipation. Broad, muscled chest, perfect washboard abs and a narrow waist leading to lean hips that disappeared beneath the waistband of low-slung jeans.

Like he could read her mind, Rafe unbuckled his belt and loosened the buttons at the top of his jeans. He moved as if he would lower the zipper, but then he changed his mind. Giving her a wicked grin, he stopped, only allowing her a peek at the black band of his boxer shorts.

"I'm not getting naked," he whispered, "until you do."

"No problem," she whispered back, and although her heart was dancing to a staccato beat, she didn't let on. Giving him a confident smile, she raised her hands to her blouse and slowly, button by button, she began to bare herself to his gaze.

His face half hidden in shadows, his eyes glinting in the glow of the shaded lamp in the corner, she could see his gaze glued to her body. She was loving it.

Still straddling his hips, Anya reached behind, her fingers moving to the clasp of her bra. Rafe sucked in his breath, just the reaction she was looking for. And if she needed any further confirmation that he wanted her, she got it soon enough. She'd sunk down onto him, her bottom finding a home on his , and what she felt there left her in no doubt that her little strip tease was working. Rafe was as hard as rock. Emboldened by the knowledge that she'd turned him on, Anya loosened the clasp and let the bra straps fall from her shoulders, and as the strip of lacy fabric tumbled down to puddle on Rafe's chest, she straightened her shoulders and arched her back, proudly presenting her breasts to his greedy gaze.

With a growl, Rafe reached for her, pulling her down until her breasts hung like succulent fruit over his mouth. As her nipple touched his lips, he sucked it into his mouth, a groan rumbling deep inside his chest.

He released her breast, and she thought it was so he could devour the other nipple, but she was wrong. He gathered her close then got up, taking her with him and then, like he was no stranger to her home, he strode down the hallway. "Your bedroom," he grunted, not pausing as he strode.

Anya's heart leaped to her throat. It was happening. She would finally know what it felt like to make love to the best man she could ever have chosen. Because, in her heart, she knew that of all the men she had ever met, Rafe was the one for her.

She wrapped her arms around his neck, then, raising her lips to his ear, she whispered, "It's the next door on the right."

When Rafe entered the room, he didn't even turn on the light. He strode to the bed, and as soon as he laid her down, his hand went to the buttons on her silk trousers. Within seconds, they were off, leaving her in nothing but the slip of cloth, the G-string she'd dared to wear. She could tell he liked it, because although the room was bathed in shadows, he paused, his hands skimming over the skimpy cloth, his bottom lip caught between his teeth. From the pale moonlight stealing in through the window, she could see him swallow, and his nostrils flare.

Then gently, almost worshipfully, he leaned over and planted a kiss on top of that strip of fabric, his lips caressing her through the cloth.

Anya gasped, and she closed her eyes, but he didn't linger. Instead, his fingers caught the strings tied at her hips and he began to pull the G-string down, slowly and seductively, inch by tortuous inch, until her most precious and private place was exposed to his gaze. She didn't move. She held her breath and closed her eyes even tighter.

When she felt Rafe slide the panties down her legs and off her feet, Anya dug her fists into the bedclothes. Still, she wouldn't open her eyes to look at him. Then, she heard him pull his zipper, and the soft rustle of clothes, and she knew jeans, boxer shorts, socks, all his clothes were now in a pile on the floor. Rafe was as naked as she was.

She sucked in her breath, drumming up the courage to sneak a peek. When she did, it was to see a man, her man, standing there, his back to her, so tall and strong, his skin so smooth, his butt so taut, that all she wanted to do was slide her palms over them.

And then, she heard the crackle. He'd opened a condom packet, and, his head down, she could imagine he was sheathing himself. Now, he was turning to face her, and before she could avert her eyes, before she could even blink, she found herself staring at his groin, at the long, stiff rod now glistening in its thin coat of latex.

Anya snapped her eyes shut again, her fingers clutching the bedclothes even tighter and this time, in addition to clenching her eyes, she bit down on her lower lip. She'd had enough of bravery for one night.

She felt when Rafe moved onto the bed, his weight making her tilt toward him, and then he lay beside her, his hand stroking her shoulder in a feather-like caress. As if to reassure her, he tickled her lips in the gentlest kiss, all the while stroking her arm, then her neck, then her breasts, his hands warming her skin until her body hummed at his caress.

As she began to relax, Rafe released her lips and slid his body lower till he was tickling her navel with the tip of his tongue. Under his ministration, she sighed, and then, as the sweet sensation spread, she began to purr, unable to stop the gentle groan of pleasure that escaped her throat.

But then, he made her plight worse. To Anya's horror, and her pleasure, Rafe left that sweet spot and slid even lower still, until his lips were skimming over her mound.

She gasped. No. He wasn't going there. Not with his tongue. Not-

"Aah." His tender touch drew the sound from her lips. He did go there, and it felt so good.

But soon, too soon, it was over, and he was sliding back up her body. And then, he was over her, inserting a knee between her legs, making them spread apart. And then he was positioning himself over her. And then he was lowering his hips.

And that was when her eyes flew open and she raised trembling hands to clutch his shoulders. "Rafe," she said, her voice an urgent whisper, "is it going to hurt?"

She was panting now, half in fright, half in anticipation, as her eyes skimmed his face.

To her dismay, that face, the same one that had just reflected such passion and desire, now froze.

"Holy shit." The words exploded from his lips even as he drew back and away from her. "What the hell are you saying?" He was up now, and off her, rolling away onto the other side of the bed. Immediately, he sat up, his eyes boring into her. "Anya. Speak to me. Are you telling me you've never done this before?"

Guilt washing over her, Anya closed her eyes, not wanting to see the disdain on his face. Suddenly feeling self-conscious, she raised her hands to cover her breasts. "It's my first time," she said softly, then bit down on her bottom lip, waiting for the axe to fall.

She felt when he punched the bed, then she heard him groan.

"Just what I need," he muttered. "I almost deflowered a virgin."

He made a decision there and then: the best thing he could do just then, was get the hell out of there before he made a move he could not reverse.

With a growl, he stumbled away and out the door.

CHAPTER FIFTEEN

WHEN RAFE GOT HOME that night, he slapped his hand against his bedroom wall. How could he have been so stupid? He knew women. He'd been with enough of them to consider himself a connoisseur. So, where this one was concerned, how could he have been so wrong?

From the first day he'd met her, he'd sort of guessed that Anya hadn't been around the block. So, she was inexperienced. That, he could live with. But a virgin?

Not that that was a bad thing; it was just that it had thrown him for a loop to find out that he would be the first. And, he had to admit, it had been a bit of a shock to find out just how innocent she really was. After all, she'd told him about going out to night clubs with her friends, sometimes going alone, getting home at four in the morning; in his mind, he'd branded her a party girl. And party girls weren't usually virgins, were they?

Well, he'd now personally run into one who was. And that taught him a good lesson – never to pass judgment on anyone.

Still kicking himself for his mistake, Rafe walked into the bathroom then stood in the shower for a long time, letting the water beat on his chest. He'd blundered when he'd made his assumption, and then he'd made things worse by the way he'd handled things. Next time he was with Anya, he would have to tread very carefully. If there was a next time...

When he got into bed, he tossed and turned, and he knew that sleep was never going to come. He glanced at the time on his cell phone. Three-thirty in the morning. God, was that all? A whole three more hours to go before the sun even poked its nose out from under the covers.

But then, as sleep usually went, Rafe didn't know when he finally drifted off. It could have been after some minutes, or it could have been hours later. The next time he knew himself was when the ringing of the cell phone jerked him awake, hauling him back to awareness.

Eyes still closed, Rafe reached over to where he knew he'd left the phone, and swiped it, ending the annoying tone. With a groan, he dragged the phone to his ear. "Hello?"

"Hey, my man. Long time. What you doing this Sunday morning? It's still morning in Germany, right?"

At the sound of Khalil's super-cheerful voice, Rafe groaned even louder. This was not what he needed after a fitful night of no sleep. "What do you want?" he growled, just wanting Khalil off the damn phone.

"Hey, is that the way to greet your best friend?" Instead of shutting up and disappearing, Khalil sounded even chirpier. "Don't tell me you were fast asleep. Do you know what time it is? Hang on. I'm online. I'll check." There was the sound of tapping on a keyboard then Khalil was back. "Right now, it's twelve forty-two in Bremen, Germany. Morning is long gone. What the blue blazes are you doing in bed at this hour?" Then, he chuckled. "No, don't tell me. My man got busy last night, right?"

Rafe's only answer was another groan.

"Hey, man, you don't sound too good." The chirp was beginning to slip from Khalil's voice even as concern began to creep in. "Are you sick or something?"

Rafe heaved a sorrowful sigh. "Yeah, I'm sick," he said, his voice heavy with disgust, "but not how you might think."

For a second, there was silence, and when Khalil's voice came again, it sounded puzzled. "I know you're not sick from a hangover. You don't drink."

"Nah," Rafe said, "that's not it."

"Then it's got to be woman problems. I know you went all the way back to Germany just to be with Anya, so your problem's gotta be with her."

Again, Rafe didn't answer. But then again, he didn't have to. Khalil was no fool. He could figure things out.

"Yeah, it's Anya," Khalil said, now sounding more certain. "But you know what? I know you and I think I know Anya well enough to say you're two sensible people. Whatever it is, if you really care for each other, you'll work it out."

Rafe couldn't help but snort. "You make it sound so easy."

"You love her, don't you?" Khalil demanded, his question like an arrow shot straight through Rafe's heart. It must have shocked him into momentary silence because Khalil asked the question again, and this time his tone was more insistent. "Don't you?"

"Yeah, I love her," he said, shifting so he could sit up in the bed. "Yes," he said again. "I love her. A lot. That's why I'm here."

"All right. Now, you're talking. That sounds like the Rafe Kent I know, a guy who's big, bad and bold, who knows what he wants and goes for it."

"All right, all right. Get to the point." Rafe knew Khalil. If he didn't cut him off fast, he'd jump on his soapbox and start preaching.

"My point, my good man, is that whatever problem you're having right now, just work it out. You're a level-headed guy. Just trust your gut. I know you'll do the right thing."

And, as it had happened so many times before, Khalil was right. The only thing to do right then was the right thing. And what that meant was, the next time he saw Anya, he had a very important decision to make.

. . ❧ . .

STUPID, STUPID, STUPID. How could she have been so stupid? Why couldn't she have kept her big mouth shut and not said a word? It wasn't like he would have known the difference. Now, he thought she'd deceived him, and for that, he probably despised her. Anya had seen it in his face. The scorn, the disgust, the annoyance. How could she face him when Monday morning came around?

And the worst part was, if he never spoke to her again, she didn't know how she would bear it. She, who had always prided herself on being strong and practical, with both feet on the ground, had, all of a sudden, turned into a wimp. And it was all the fault of the man who'd waltzed into her school and into her life. He was like no other man she'd ever met...because he was the man who had stolen her heart.

And that was why she'd wanted him to be the one who would take her on that ultimate journey to womanhood. Except that he'd turned her down. Flat.

Deflated and depressed, Anya spent most of Sunday moping around the house, hoping Rafe would get over his anger and just call her. And then, she'd spent the other part of Sunday peeved with him. After all, what right did he have to be angry with her simply because she hadn't been the type to sleep around? Wasn't that a good thing? She had a good mind never to speak to him again.

And that was why, when her phone rang that evening and she saw that it was Rafe, her heart leaped for joy, but then her brain kicked into gear, reminding her that right now she was not in the mood to speak to that man. And that was why she stared at the phone and let it ring until the call went to voicemail.

An hour later, the phone rang again, and when she saw it was Rafe, just like last time, her heart went tumbling over itself, eager to answer and hear his voice again. Thank God for her sensible brain to rein in that giddy heart and sit on it till it calmed its crazy self down. No, she would not be speaking to Rafe Kent that Sunday, or her name wasn't Anya Petersen.

But by Monday morning, that campaign was a lost cause. She was dying to see Rafe again. Eager as a beaver, she headed out to work early, hoping he'd be early, too, so they would get a chance to talk. Now that she'd slept on it, she realized that he'd probably just been surprised. Maybe he wasn't angry at all. If he'd been peeved, he definitely would not have been calling her all Sunday afternoon.

But when she got to the school, Rafe was nowhere to be seen. Disappointed, she dragged herself off to her class. She could only take consolation in the fact that she would see him in the staff room after classes ended that day.

As soon as the final bell rang that afternoon, Anya packed up her materials and hurried off to the staff room, happy that she would finally lay eyes on the man who had made her heart so light that it made her feel like she was floating like a feather. This was the kind of thing she used to read in romance novels, and each time she'd rolled her eyes in disbelief, but now it was happening to her. Those magical feelings were actually real. If it hadn't happened to her, she never would have believed it.

Anya plopped her supplies on top of her desk and sat down to wait for Rafe to show up. And she waited. And she waited. Where the heck was he?

The other teachers tried to engage her in chit-chat, but she was so distracted, they finally gave up. It was only when she saw Claire walk in that she felt a surge of relief. Immediately, she walked over to the woman's desk and greeted her with a smile. "Hi, Claire. Is everything okay with your assistant? I haven't seen him all day. Rumor has it that you have him locked away in the junior kindergarten closet." She was trying to make a joke, but it didn't come out quite like one. She sounded too perturbed for it to be a joke.

"Didn't he tell you?" Claire asked, regarding her with curiosity. "He called me yesterday to say he had to head back to the United States. He left yesterday evening." She frowned. "I thought for sure he would have called you."

The shock was like a swift sting to her heart. "No, he didn't," she said, her voice choked up. "He..." and then she stopped. Yes, he did. He'd called her four times yesterday, and she hadn't picked up, not even once. She'd been so bent on punishing him.

And then the more important part of what Claire said sank in. "He's gone back to the United States? But why?"

Claire's brows knitted in a frown. "It's his father," she said. "He suddenly fell ill. Rafe had to rush back home to be with him." She shook her head. "He sounded really worried. I hope everything will be all right."

"I hope so, too," Anya murmured, feeling sick to her stomach. What had she done? Rafe had been trying to reach her to tell her about his father and she'd totally ignored him. Now, he was gone back to the States, thinking she was callous and unfeeling, ignoring him at a time when he needed a friend. She felt so low, she didn't know what to do with herself.

She had to find him. "Did he leave a number where we could reach him while he's away?"

"No, dear, he didn't give me one," Claire said. "Mrs. Coleman would probably have all his personal information on file, but you know that's confidential. She would never divulge any of that information to either one of us."

Slowly, Anya nodded. "I know. I just wish he'd told you..." her voice trailed off as she realized there was something she could do. Rafe was a businessman and he'd spoken as if his company was fairly large. He was bound to show up if she entered his name in the Google search engine.

Tonight, when she got home, she would do just that. She would not stop until she found Rafe again.

CHAPTER SIXTEEN

THANK GOD.

As soon as Rafe stepped outside the door of the hospital room, leaving his mother and brothers with his father, he walked over to an empty seat in the waiting room and slumped into it.

It had been a false alarm. Now, he could breathe a sigh of relief. He'd seen his dad, and he was going to be all right.

Reaching his hand up, he raked his fingers through his hair, remembering the shock of hearing that his father had been rushed to the emergency room with a heart attack. That Sunday had been the worst day of his life. It started out terribly wrong as he pondered the way he'd handled the situation with Anya, and then, just when he'd decided to call her and straighten things out, he'd gotten that call, the one that made his stomach plummet.

Immediately, he'd arranged a flight out of Germany, and then he'd called Anya to tell her he had to go. At least, he'd tried, two times from the apartment, once on the way to the airport, and even from the plane. But every time, no answer. It was as if, for her, he'd ceased to exist.

But he would give it another try. Now that his father was out of the woods, he could think again, and the first person he thought of was Anya.

He dialed the number to her cell phone and this time, although it was almost ten o'clock at night in Bremen, she picked up on the second ring. He didn't even get a chance to greet her.

"Rafe, are you all right?" she asked, her voice concerned and breathless. "Claire told me what happened. How is your father?" The questions tumbled out in a rush, and Rafe could tell she was distraught.

"He's fine," he said, quickly reassuring her. "It was a false alarm. Everybody thought it was a heart attack but when they rushed him to the ER, the doctors found it was acid reflux. He's resting now. He'll be okay."

"*Mein Gott*," she whispered, "I was so scared for you. And I wanted to call you. I found a US phone number, but I only got your office. They weren't...too friendly."

Rafe sighed. Best to come clean. "I'm sorry, Anya. They're a bit defensive. You wouldn't be the first woman to call the office asking for me."

"And I can guess why." Now, her voice took on a slightly harder edge. "At what point in our relationship were you going to tell me you're a billionaire? I had to go on Google to find that out?"

Rafe grimaced. He hoped Anya wasn't going to make a big deal out of this. "That's not important," he said, his voice firm. "Do you know what's important? The fact that you're a stubborn little..." he paused. He'd almost called her a little cuss again, but he knew that would only distract her. "You're a stubborn little girl I owed a spanking from way back, and now I owe you another one for not answering your damn phone. Do you know how many messages I left you?"

"I know. I'm sorry." Her voice was suitably contrite. "I didn't check the messages until Monday, after Claire told me what happened. It was because I was so upset with you. That was childish of me. I'm sorry."

"Not as sorry as you're going to be when I get back," he said, his voice terse with his unveiled threat. "I don't like the idea of you living alone, what with crazies like your neighbor's husband running around town. Like it or not, as soon as I get back,, you're living with me."

"Living with you?" She repeated the words like she was confused. "But I have a house already." Then she paused, and when she spoke again, her voice was low. "Are you moving in with me?"

Rafe gave a hiss of exasperation. She was usually a sharp-witted girl, but now she was being so slow. "Anya Petersen," he said slowly, "what part of 'will you marry me' don't you understand?"

She gasped. And then she shrieked into the phone, making him jump. "I'm going to kill you," she screeched. "Just wait till you get back. Is that the way you propose?"

Rafe grimaced again. "Sorry, Anya. That's just my way, I guess. When I get back to Germany, I'll get down on one knee and do it right." Then ,he chuckled. "Heck, I'll do it right in the middle of my classroom full of babies, if you want. For now, though, just understand that you will be marrying me when I get back."

"It sounds like you're under the mistaken impression that you're in charge." He could hear the laughter in Anya's voice.

"I am in charge."

"No, you're not, and when you get back, I'll prove it. I have this hold where I put my fingers just at the base of your throat and-"

"Woman, will you just shut up and tell me you'll marry me?"

That only made her laugh out loud. "How can I shut up and speak at the same time?"

Rafe shook his head then heaved a sigh of utter frustration. "Anya, Anya, Anya." He sighed again. "Anya, will you marry me?"

"Of course, I will, Rafe." Then, her voice turned sly. "As long as you admit that I'm the one in charge."

Rafe sighed yet again. "Yes, Anya. You're the one in charge." He shook his head. "Boy, you've changed. What happened to the sweet girl I met?" Then, he chuckled. "Anything to make you happy. You're in charge."

"See, that wasn't so hard, was it?" She chuckled into the phone. "But there's one more thing."

"Yes, Anya," he said, resigned to more of her foolishness. "What is it?"

"You still owe me two spankings, and I expect you to deliver."

Now that, he could handle. "With pleasure, my little bully," he said. "I can hardly wait."

EPILOGUE

ONE YEAR LATER, ANYA was big, bulging and beaming. Whoever said pregnancy was hard work didn't know what they were talking about. She'd never felt better, or more energetic, in her life. She had a wide smile on her face as she sat with friends and family in the living room of the house Rafe had bought them, right there in Bremen. Rafe, ever the caring husband, had arranged a surprise baby shower so that the people they loved could share in their joy.

Now, he was leaning over to whisper in her ear. "I can sneak out now, right? Baby showers are for women. Lion and Khalil and me, we want to-"

"Sit," she whispered back, through clenched teeth. "Don't you move one inch." And then, like she hadn't just bullied her husband, she smiled and waved at her fellow teacher. "It's beautiful, Claire. And yellow is always a safe color for babies." Then, while the rest of the group oohed and aahed over baby clothes, she waved Rafe's friends over. "I heard the business you guys set up is going pretty well," she said.

"Sure is." Lion was grinning from ear to ear. "With the business advice we get from your good husband, we'll be rich in no time."

Khalil laughed. "I wouldn't make big plans just yet, but we'll do fine. We're off to a pretty good start."

And then, as the guests began to drift toward the buffet table, Rafe gave Anya a nudge. "Are you going to tell them now?"

She nodded. "Now is as good a time as any."

With Rafe's help, she heaved up and out of her chair. "Ladies and gentlemen," she called out, "I have an announcement to make."

Everyone paused and turned to look at her and she was suddenly overwhelmed with gratitude for the love these people were showing her, some of them traveling thousands of miles just to wish her well. All three of Rafe's brothers were there – Ransom and Ryder and Ridge – and so were her mom and dad. And then there were friends from all over, including many of the teachers from her school.

"This was quite a surprise," she said, "and I have to thank my husband for getting all of you to come to celebrate with me today." She turned to look at Rafe. "To celebrate our family."

Then, she turned back to her audience. "And now, I have a surprise for you."

That got their attention. They were all staring at her in anticipation.

"I appreciate all the gifts you brought," she said, her smile widening. "They will be put to good use. Double time." She reached over and took Rafe's hand and pulled him over to stand by her side. "Rafe and I wanted to keep this a secret until the very last, but you've all been so sweet. I have to share the good news." She paused, watching their eager faces, enjoying torturing them with the suspense. But then, she relented.

"Rafe and I are expecting twins. A boy and a girl."

That brought the house down. The cheers made her feel like a celebrity. But those cheers were not for her. They were for the stars of the show, her babies. And she knew they were hearing it all.

And in the middle of the applause, she turned to reward her husband with a kiss. "Thank you for my babies," she whispered.

But Khalil, who'd been standing close by, seemed to have heard every word. He gave them a quirky smile, and, never one to be shy, declared, "He should be the one thanking you for his perfect gifts. Babies for the billionaire."

"True word," Rafe said, and he and his friend bumped fists with him.

And, loving it, all Anya could do was laugh.

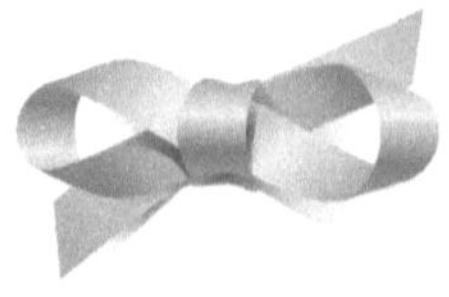

Thank you for reading!

BABIES FOR THE BILLIONAIRE

Sneak Preview for the next in the series:
THE BILLIONAIRE BROTHERS KENT
Book 3

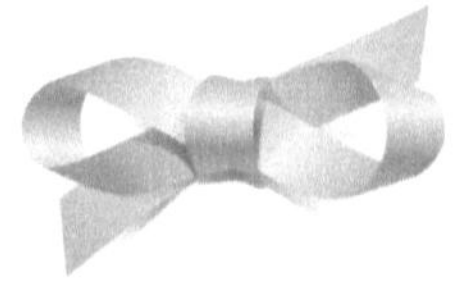

Billionaire's Blackmail Bride
CHAPTER ONE

SWEET. THE GODS MUST be smiling down on him today. Lani Donatelli was sitting right here in his office and she was in big trouble. Could things go any better?

Leaning back in his chair, Ridge tented his fingers and regarded her through narrowed eyes. He was going to play tough even though he was laughing inside. She'd fallen right into his hands and he could not believe his luck.

"How's that again?" he asked, feigning confusion, watching the emotions flit across her face.

Lani gave an exasperated sigh. "Ridge Kent, you heard every word I said. Why should I repeat myself?" The color rising in her cheeks, Lani was clenching and unclenching her hands like she was trying hard not to hop out of her chair, reach across the desk and strangle him. She looked so cute when she was angry, like a little pink pixie, so tiny she could pass for a kid as she sat there, lost in the big, black office chair. And it didn't help that she was sporting a super-short boy haircut. If he didn't already know her he'd swear she was a stray twelve year old who'd wandered into his office.

But enough of admiring little Miss Cuteness. She'd asked a pointed question and he was only too willing to answer. "Maybe you should repeat yourself," he said, his tone cool, "because you really need this favor."

At his words Lani's eyes shot daggers and she looked like if she could have killed him with her glare she would have. "You don't need to rub it in," she said through clenched teeth.

"Oh, but I do," he replied. "I most certainly do."

"Jerk," she muttered under her breath.

But that didn't faze him at all. He knew exactly what he was doing. "I'm waiting," he said, just in case she needed a little more prompting.

Lani gave a heavy sigh then shook her head. "I'll go slower this time just so you'll understand. I've lost my funding for the research project I'm working on. A very important project. It's impossible for me to find alternative funding at such short notice and that's why I need your help."

"I see." Ridge leaned forward, holding her gaze. "And what's so important about this research project of yours? Why not shelve it and move on to something else?"

She looked at him like he was just short of being a blinking idiot. "Don't you get it? This is important. Life changing. It could make a difference in thousands of people's lives. You don't start a study that could make such an impact and then you shelve it. Are you crazy?"

For someone who'd come to his door begging she sure wasn't acting humble. The way she was speaking to him it was like he was the one who needed the favor, not her. Ridge had to hold in a chuckle. He kept his face serious as he asked the next question. "So if your project is that important why can't you get funding? Isn't this the sort of thing those big pharmaceutical companies want to be involved in?"

Lani grimaced. "Not this one. I'm not doing research on a synthetic drug, something they can patent. My research is on natural plant alternatives so they don't give a damn. If you can't make billions off it they don't want to hear about it."

"I see," he said again, nodding slowly as he pondered her words. "So what you're saying is, you want me to invest in a project for which there is no return. The pharmaceutical companies won't do it so why should I?"

"Why should... is that all you ever think about? How much money you stand to make?"

Her scowl was so dark Ridge was having a hard time keeping a straight face. God, he was having fun pushing her buttons.

He shrugged. "I'm a businessman," he said, his tone nonchalant. "If you ain't makin' money you ain't got no business."

That got her good. He could see it in the way her teeth clenched and her eyes narrowed. "Well, if that's the position you're going to take it looks like I came to the wrong person." She slapped her hands on the arms of her chair and hopped to her feet. "Thanks for nothing. Good day, Mr. Kent." Then she turned and stalked off toward the door.

Ridge waited until her hand was on the knob and then he spoke. "Come back here, Miss Donatelli." His voice was firm and curt. "Come back and sit down," he paused for maximum effect, "or else you're not getting a cent out of me."

She froze, hand still on the knob, and then slowly she turned and stared back at him. Eyes narrowed, she frowned. "So, you're giving me the money?"

Ridge gave her a crooked grin. "I might. But there's just one thing."

Her frown deepened and, moving slowly, she folded her arms in front of her. "What," she said slowly, the word dripping with suspicion, "thing?"

She was curious now, and wary, but he wasn't going to make things that easy. Lani would have to learn that he was the one holding the blade and she'd better tread carefully.

"I'll tell you," he said, his tone frigid, "as soon as you find your butt back in your chair."

He saw her quick look of surprise at his imperious tone but in a flash it was gone. Now her ebony eyes glinted with unmistakable anger. It was obvious she wanted to tell him to go to hell but she was too smart for that. Her mind was ticking fast and he could see the second that she decided to suck it up and do what he'd ordered. She was a proud and independent woman but she wasn't stupid.

With a twist of her lips she released her arms and marched back to the chair she'd just vacated. It was a good thing she was wearing slacks and not a dress because she practically flung herself down into it, her expression telling him that whatever it was he had to say to her, she was not looking forward to it.

"So what 'thing' is it you want to tell me," she said, "before you give me the money?"

Ridge didn't answer. He'd been planning to make her a friendly proposition, one she could live with, but screw that. Little Miss Lani was being a bit too haughty for his liking...even though she was the one asking favors. Time to take her down a notch or two.

"I'll give you the money," he said, his eyes never leaving hers, "on one condition."

Lani drew in a slow breath and her gaze grew even more suspicious. "What condition?"

"You can get your money to do your precious research project," he said, his tone even, "as long as you agree to marry me. I want you to be my wife for a year."

That declaration didn't get him the reaction he'd been expecting. Instead of the shock and horror he'd anticipated Lani did the very opposite. The contrary girl burst out laughing.

"I heard you could be a joker, but this takes the cake. So you're a businessman turned comedian now?" She wasn't shy with her guffaws. She was laughing so hard Ridge was thinking she might pitch forward and fall out of her chair.

But he wouldn't say a word. He would let her have her moment of fun and then he would set her straight. That grin would be wiped from her face soon enough.

When she finally calmed down enough to stop laughing and slide back in her chair Ridge got up and walked over to the credenza on top of which sat an ice bucket with bottles of water and juice. He glanced over at her. "Want one?" he asked.

She shook her head.

With a shrug he turned, grabbed a bottle of water and tipped it to his lips. He downed a third of it in one swig. As he lowered the bottle and replaced the cap he regarded her with casual interest. "Ready to talk to me now?"

"About what?" she asked, a smile teasing the corner of her mouth. "Of course you weren't serious."

He gave her a slow smile. "I'm dead serious."

It was only then that things seemed to sink in for Lani. The smile that had tickled her mouth disappeared. The lips that had just curled so prettily now turned thin and firm. "But why?" she asked, her tone half combative, half confused. "Why would you want me to marry you? We don't even like each other."

And the way she said the last sentence, curling her lips like the very thought repulsed her, made him even more determined to stick to his guns. He would bring her to heel if it killed him.

"Let's just say I've got my reasons." He spoke calmly, not giving away the fact that she'd just pissed him off. There would be time enough to get his revenge for that transgression.

"But I don't get it." As he walked back to his desk her eyes followed him, boring into him, never letting him go. He definitely had her attention now. "Ever since we met," she continued, "we've been at loggerheads. In fact, I wouldn't even be in your office right now if I weren't desperate."

Ridge smiled. "That, little Lani, is the operative word. The question is, how desperate are you?" He made sure to put emphasis on the word just so she didn't miss the point.

Lani's breathing was growing more and more agitated by the minute. Nostrils flaring, she got up and out of the chair and stood there, hands clenched at her sides. "You're sick. You know that?"

His smile deepened. "I may be," he said, his tone relaxed as ever, "but you're the one who's going to make this decision. Not me."

With a shrug he sank back into his chair and looked at the seething woman standing in front of his desk. "My condition is on the table, Lani. Take it or leave it."

• • ❧ • •

To read more about Lani and Ridge, get your copy of 'Billionaire's Blackmail Bride' from your favorite online retailer.

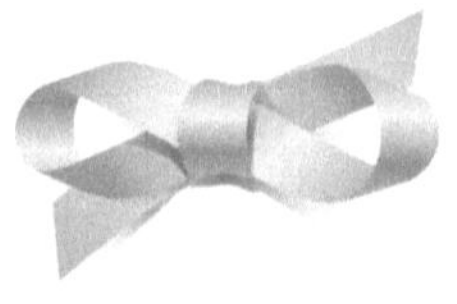

THE BILLIONAIRE BROTHERHOOD

Volume 1 - Tamed by the Billionaire

Volume 2 - Maid in the USA

Volume 3 - Billionaire's Island Bride

Volume 4 - Dangerous Deception

Volume 5 - To Tame a Tycoon

Volume 6 - Sweet Seduction

Volume 7 - Daddy by December

Volume 8 - To Catch a Man (in 30 Days or Less)

Volume 9 – Bedding her Billionaire Boss

Volume 10 - Her Indecent Proposal

Volume 11 - So Much Trouble When She Walked In

Volume 12 – Married by Midnight

THE BILLIONAIRE BROTHERS KENT

Book 1 - The Billionaire Next Door
Book 2 - Babies for the Billionaire
Book 3 - Billionaire's Blackmail Bride
Book 4 - Bossing the Billionaire

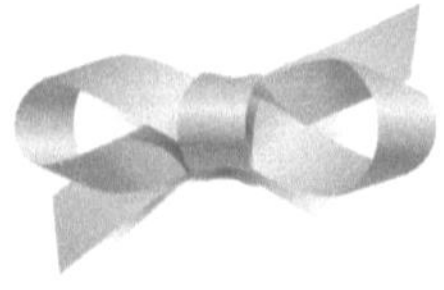

THE CASTILLOS

HOLIDAY EDITIONS

Rome for the Holidays (Novella)
Rome for Always (Novel)

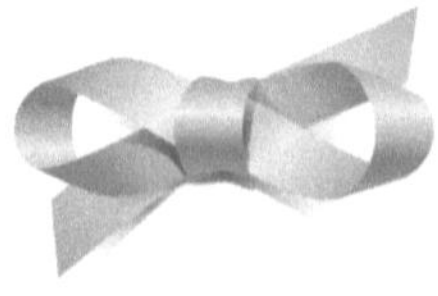

The NAUGHTY AND NICE Series

Volume 1 - **Naughty by Nature**

COMEDY, CONFLICT & ROMANCE
Series

Book 1 - Taming the Fury
Book 2 - Outwitting the Wolf
Book 3 - Romancing Malone

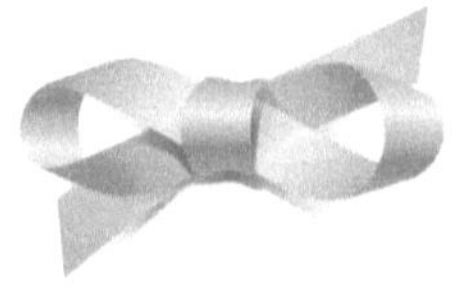

THE BILLIONAIRE BACHELORETTES OF BEL-AIR

Book 1 -In Bed with the Enemy

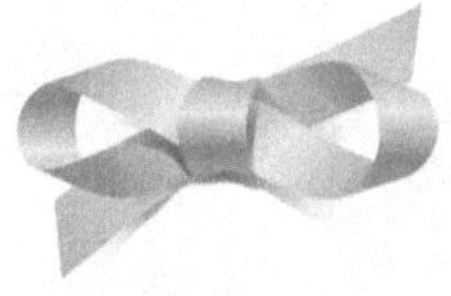

NOVELLAS

The Billionaire's Bold Bet
Tamed by the Billionaire - The Sequel

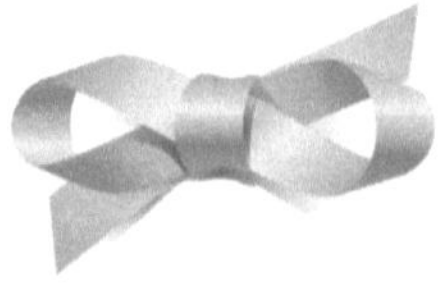

MADE FOR THE MOVIES

Trading Spaces

Back from the Future

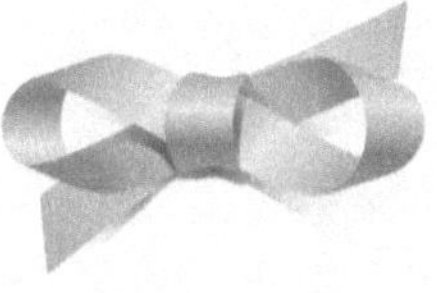

COLLABORATIONS

A is for Arrangement – Eden Adams

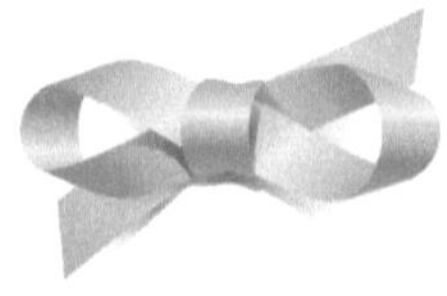

INTERNATIONAL

SPA - Domado por el Multimillionario
FRE - La Milliardaire Apprivoisee
SPA - Romance de la Criada en los EU
FRE - En Amour avec la Femme de Chambre
GER - Vom Milliardar Gezahmt
SPA - La Novia Cautiva del Multimillionario
SPA - Engano Peligroso
JAP - For titles in Japanese, contact Tuttle Mori Agency, Tokyo

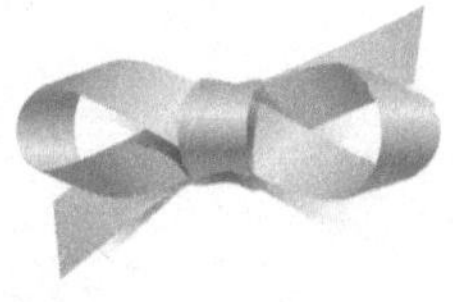

NONFICTION

How to Write a Romance Novel

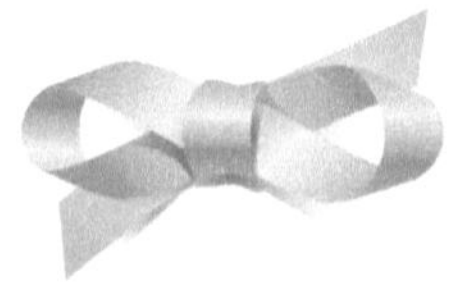

COLLECTIONS

THE BILLIONAIRE BROTHERHOOD, Coll. I - Vols. 1 - 4

THE BILLIONAIRE BROTHERHOOD, Coll. II - Vols. 5 - 8

THE BILLIONAIRE BROTHERHOOD, Coll. III - Vols. 9 - 12

BILLIONAIRE BROS. KENT - Books 1 - 4

THE BILLIONAIRE BROTHERHOOD DOUBLE COLLECTION - Vols. 1 - 8

THE BILLIONAIRE BROTHERHOOD MEGA-COLLECTION - Vols. 1 - 12

THE BILLIONAIRE BROTHERS KENT - Vols. 1 - 4

THE CASTILLOS - Vols. 1 - 4

COMEDY, CONFLICT & ROMANCE - Vols. 1 - 3

HOME for the HOLIDAYS - Vols. 1 - 3

AUDIO BOOKS

Available from your favorite retailers and libraries

Tamed by the Billionaire

Maid in the USA

Billionaire's Island Bride

Dangerous Deception

Bedding Her Billionaire Boss

Her Indecent Proposal

BABIES FOR THE BILLIONAIRE

So Much Trouble When She Walked In
Married by Midnight
Rome for the Holidays
Billionaire's Blackmail Bride
How to Write a Romance Novel

. . ⸂⸃ . .

Author contact:
judyangeloauthor@gmail.com

. . ⸂⸃ . .

For updates on books,
and my 'Pay It Forward' Charity Program,
visit|
judyangelo.blogspot.com[1]
USING MY BOOKS EACH MONTH TO SUPPORT A WORTHY CAUSE

---

1. http://judyangelo.blogspot.com/

Don't miss out!

Visit the website below and you can sign up to receive emails whenever JUDY ANGELO publishes a new book. There's no charge and no obligation.

https://books2read.com/r/B-A-WPD-EFEC

BOOKS 2 READ

Connecting independent readers to independent writers.

Did you love *Babies for the Billionaire*? Then you should read *Billionaire's Captive Island Bride (Dare's Story)*[2] by JUDY ANGELO!

BAD BOY BILLIONAIRE VERSUS REBEL ISLAND BRIDE - AND THE WINNER IS...

Normally shy and reserved, college student Erin Samuels goes to the island of Santa Marta where she breaks out of her shell and does things that shock even her. And, as if that weren't bad enough, she ends up trapped in a marriage by blackmail!

Dare DeSouza is used to women throwing themselves at him and he lumps Erin Samuels in the same category. Gold-diggers, that's what they all are, but this time he has a plan. He sets out to teach Erin a lesson she'll never forget...and ends up learning the greatest lesson of his life.

---

2. https://books2read.com/u/3npJR4

3. https://books2read.com/u/3npJR4

An island romance that will keep readers guessing every step of the way...

Read more at judyangelo.blogspot.com.

Also by JUDY ANGELO

Bad Boy Billionaires - Where Are They Now?
Tamed by the Billionaire - The Sequel

Billionaire Bachelorettes of Bel-Air
In Bed with the Enemy

Billionaire Brotherhood
The Billionaire Brotherhood III, Vols. 9 - 12

Historias Multimillionarias para Navidad
Rome para Navidad

KNOWLEDGE in a NUTSHELL
How to Write a Romance Novel

MADE FOR THE MOVIES Fantasy Romance
Trading Spaces
Back from the Future
Back from the Future with BONUS Trading Spaces

Multimillonarios Machos
Domada por el Multimillionario
Domado por el Multimillionario, Bilingual Version

The BAD BOY BILLIONAIRES Series
To Tame a Tycoon
Sweet Seduction
Daddy by December
To Catch a Man (in 30 Days or Less)
Bedding Her Billionaire Boss
Her Indecent Proposal
So Much Trouble When She Walked In
Married by Midnight
Bad Boy Billionaires - Collection II, Vols. 5 - 8
Bad Boy Billionaires Mega-Collection Vols 1 - 12

THE BILLIONAIRE BROTHERHOOD
Tamed by the Billionaire (Roman's Story)
Maid in the USA (Pierce's Story)
Billionaire's Captive Island Bride (Dare's Story)
Dangerous Deception (Storm's Story)

The Billionaire Brotherhood Coll. III Bks 9 - 12
The Billionaire Brotherhood Collection I, Vols. 1 - 4
The Billionaire Brotherhood Double Coll. Bks. 1 - 8

The Billionaire Brothers Kent
The Billionaire Next Door
Babies for the Billionaire
Billionaire's Blackmail Bride
Bossing the Billionaire
The Billionaire Brothers Kent

The BILLIONAIRE HOLIDAY Series
Rome for the Holidays
Rome for Always
Home for the Holidays

The Castillos
Beauty and the Beastly Billionaire
Training the Tycoon
The Mogul's Maiden Mistress
Eva and the Extreme Executive
The Castillos - The Collection

The Comedy, Conflict and Romance Series
Taming the Fury
Outwitting the Wolf

Romancing Malone
Comedy, Confict & Romance - The Collection

The Naughty and Nice Series
Naughty by Nature

Standalone
The Billionaire's Bold Bet

Watch for more at judyangelo.blogspot.com.